MW00413992

PROPER NAME

& Other Stories

ALSO AVAILABLE FROM NEW DIRECTIONS

A Bernadette Mayer Reader

Bernadette Mayer

PROPER NAME

& Other Stories

A NEW DIRECTIONS BOOK

Copyright © 1996, 1995, 1994, 1992 by Bernadette Mayer

All rights reserved. Except for brief passages quoted in a newspaper, magazine, radio, or television review, no part of this book may be reproduced in any form or by any means, electronic or mechanical, including photocopying and recording, or by any information storage and retrieval system, without permission in writing from the Publisher.

Manufactured in the United States of America
New Directions Books are printed on acid-free paper
First published as New Directions Paperbook 824 in 1996
Published simultaneously in Canada by Penguin Books Canada Limited

Library of Congress Cataloging-in-Publication Data

Mayer, Bernadette.
    Proper name & other stories / Bernadette Mayer.
        p.   cm. — (New Directions paperbook ; 824)
    ISBN 0–8112–1325–0 (alk. paper)
    1. Manners and customs—Fiction.   I. Title.
PS3563.A952P76   1996   818'.5409—dc20   95–53735
                                                                           CIP

Celebrating 60 years of publishing
for James Laughlin
by New Directions Publishing Corporation
80 Eighth Avenue, New York 10011

TABLE OF CONTENTS

a   red
b   pink
c   tan
d   black
e   green
f   blue gray
g   brown
h   gray-blue
i   gray
j   light brown
k   dark blue
l   gray
m   brown
n   gray
o   white
p   blue-purple
q   gold
r   orange-red
s   yellow
t   blue-gray
u   gray
v   gray-purple
w   light brown
x   darker brown
y   yellow-gold
z   brown

AGORAPHOBIA

There was a space in the streets that was arrogant when she was born. Dream up a pride that will be his own: ''I am overhigh.''

To begin with to begin over, to do it again, not having learned any lessons the first or the hundredth time: if nothing else, I cannot shun the title. These are my children, I adore them.

My daughters are my pride.

I am inspired, I am the pride of all the poets, flowering. There is indeed magnificence in this as it is my sexual desire, that subject being its own prime. I am blinded, wounded, conquered. I am still high. I am on my mettle. I am taking this brief chance to tell you before that spirit is caught.

I did not mean to begin with such exactness and courage, I thought to myself I am perhaps also the snake, the metropolitan demon. I take clues to what I will see, who is that at the door now?

No one walks in, no man or woman is entering. This is high-toned, does it need to be so? After all, a man or woman is walking about somewhere, perhaps knocking, perhaps finishing his or her entrance at some door, threatening. There is a murder, followed by hilarious bouts of laughter.

A sudden wind catches me, I may be pregnant again. Or by the sun, carrying twins. "She could not bear the trauma of childbirth, she must not become pregnant."

And as the light in the room becomes more yellow with the storm: "She gave the baby milk as she had seen her mother do, but not enough, the baby died."

Someone's here, no, someone's here, make them laugh hilariously again, then, adhere precariously to the most perfect structure: a metalliferous streak in the stone, a proliferation of writers yielding no one's road where, where the Hrubiec Orchards may be seen. Memory's part. And a signal from the voice at the door, even before she really opens it to admit me, saying: there is nothing special about this award, don't let it go to your head.

I am Little Hot Spot. And no and in the search for a proper tone, the decorousness of the east, good humor of the west, I have perhaps abandoned my man. This is something I am working on. I see black, I see the eye doctor.

To win praise and its adornments, I would journey alone on the road without exits. To speak easily of myself, I would lie on the flat roof in winter where no snow melts. I would sweep my own roof with a broom. I would actively penetrate the character I will create.

What will come? Freud sitting alone denying himself even the abstinence he craves, what will he be able to do about it? About what? About the farce I will make of fear, in my own earnestness and in my desire to please.

Is there something else left to say? A time like a wind blows around too quickly and its exact memories escape me. Even the direction is vague in the hills. Now the voice changes.

Town of Worthington, everybody off! There I saw a magpie, no, I saw yellow leaves, Lewis went to get the anti-freeze, I went out into the big field scared. I thought I would never get back again, back to the big house. Bigger than the house, the field looked smaller because it became black.

And there I saw that washing clothes in a big tub and all by hand was a way to ease the symptoms of the great police truck that was seizing my heart, leaving its black thumbprints all over it. Take it off! Run lots of cold water over it.

I wait and disobey. I do it against the Catholic priests who are waiting prissy in the confessional, also to wash me. There's really so little to do as a sin, one kneeling. Did you ever see the boy who elevated himself during prayer? The greatest sinners become the greatest saints, and so on. But I would never harm the baby!

What is imagination? Your mother looks like a bird, your father Aristotle Onassis. You are just a plum who fell from the sky.

But I didn't need to say that, that was off the subject. He is a severe man at times, she is an innocent child. The heart can be something to sell, only in exchange for rapture.

The streets are tents, my panic is an enigma, the day is so crowded and who is my friend? Who is the man who recognizes me? What is true feeling? Whom can I trust? This man, walking down the hill, so weak and skinny and dismal? Is it he?

I shouldn't have dared to say that. The hill is so high and deserted, the children so heavy. "I am afraid of walking downhill."

That is something else, I can see that. The park is an oven today, frying the snow into soup, good soup. If ever a watch were a collar, it's under that pine-needle tree. Wait, I'm mincing words. What pie? Ever graduate a demon? A nomad?

Now it's all over, a big let-down. I made it. The weather is stark and realistically this snow is an average amount though it's been torture, though it's given me a chance to be alone and speak in the voice it's given me, for much longer. My house is my site. What I mean is it sits on my past and therefore there is a strictness about it which causes today to have all the color and the feeling of a day twelve years ago and leaves me tomorrow then even so much older than I am, old enough to have a sudden death, a sudden weakness, a thinning out then, a closeness with the affliction from the prevailing winds.

Every slow or fast wind is a whole country. The country of India where like the Indian woman I am giving birth to 25 babies a minute, but wait, but have I waited too long? If my timing is perfect, will the rest of my activities be off?

Am I ceasing to be human or pretending not to hear? The agoraphobe is human as a lion. But if my race were as infrequent as the lion's race, no hunger could leave me so cold as the marketplace. Sleep baby sleep, the cottage vale is deep, the little lamb is on the green with woolly fleece so soft and clean . . .

Sleep baby sleep.

Two babies seem to sleep one afternoon. I nurse one baby, I do not feel unseemly. If a fear can be special then you do not have a heart. Sleep peace and quiet quiet sleep.

Perhaps those you can rely on all fall ill. There was a case of sleeplessness, a young girl fell ill with pneumonia, a man with a kidney stone, two hairdressers in an automobile accident, a young woman who proved to be off balance. There's a child who speaks a foreign language, two children, two bilingual blond children, each has another world which is doubled.

I don't know everything. One of the children is watching me. Could it be inherited? Or breathed from the air I expel? A penchant, a tendency due to a propinquity. What gives a person to stand in this way? Between my mother and myself stands the rest of this ratio of children. If I am identical to her then my younger daughter becomes equivalent to me.

There was a moment in the enclosed yard, windless. A girl walked down, out and over to the ramp, back past the post office mindlessly. I asked her a question. It was the sound of a voice bouncing off snow. "There are three ways out of the yard: which should or must we use?" She didn't have the answer nor did she guess that there was a riddle. She was a visitor.

The stairway with its single bannister is a way to form words. It is a closed space, you are neither outside nor in. You cannot call, you cannot check, the inside walls are also brick. It is soundless sometimes, it is some form of singing for a woman, something like humming. Each step, each step, the big red boot on the foot. Yet the child is not made less or less human by accompanying me. Guess what she is thinking, it isn't literal.

There is an element in panic which is akin to childhood: it is a way of checking skills through memory and repetition. I will see now if I can still do that and what it feels like, or, I will see if I can still not do that. It's the entire nursery rhyme from start to finish: Elsie Marley's grown so fine she won't get up to feed the swine but lies in bed till eight or nine, lazy Elsie Marley.

There will be buttons on my coat, willy-nilly: "Let's get out of here!" Peace in the valley for me. And that's the rhythm of it, roll and rest, you must rest an unselfconscious rest.

Remember I begged you to tie me to the bed so I wouldn't be able to sleep with my feet out the window of the 17th floor? Remember the distance from the house to the road with nothing but woods in between? Or going into the swamp? Have we ever gone up a mountain together? On foot? There's the fascination of what it would feel like, most likely death would not come and we envision that.

In solitary the men and women are watched. To Emma Goldman it was the torture of living with strangers by force. This man or woman does what he or she has to do. We put off doing the laundry, the small town becomes even smaller, in New York everyone's crazy anyway. You get into a taxi without a realistic fear.

Remember the episode of the cave? I watched them all crawl in, one behind the other, hearing their voices slowly fade away. Two came out early, I wouldn't go in. Remember that same year fording the Massachusetts river? There was a human chain and some lost their footing and had to swim downstream. There was a man who would say, "As long as you're with me, nothing bad can happen."

Only I am listening now, my ears are pricked up. Another Edgar Poe with the darkness of the hearts of those male writers: she was an invalid, or, she never left her room. She became a recluse. Sophia was confined to her room until she married Nathaniel. "They never went out in the east wind."

This inventory of my quarantine is pending your approval. My appetite is better but you must be the judge of that. Just let me say that I could eat a horse or a house, eat us out of house and home, eat a sandwich of mountains, a stew of whole towns. Would I then be truly lonely without this edge onto the precipice of isolation which is divine?

Here are the wrappings for you to unravel, each layer in itself like the famous Chinese box.

How many days has my baby to play? Saturday Sunday Monday Tuesday Wednesday Thursday Friday Saturday Sunday and Monday. One two three o'clock four o'clock the wind is blowing madly, everything is white, whiter, it's today's second storm and this one's madder, you can't see across the street, it's snowing furiously, my fate is sealed. It's Friday and the traffic goes by anyway, up and down the street. Boys are throwing snowballs in the park, there are footprints in the yard, small yard attached to the house, yard with three ways out, yard surrounded by a high brick wall, the space between the wall and the sky, park across the street, wide open space of it, sitting in the corner, sitting in the snow, in the grass, free-wheeling sitting, am I visible? Down Cliffwood is too far, down to Holliston a hundred miles, car that went to the junk-yard, it's better to take the car, little closed space of it, big front seat, nervy driving, you drove into a rock, you drove into a ditch, then I drove and the gas came too fast and the car broke, you put your foot right through the floorboard, there's a big hole in the tailpipe, the car flipped around on the icy road and wound up facing the other way, I was sliding all over the place, the road gets no sun, I shouldn't have used the brakes. The wind blows, life is neat, many people are coming and going, in and out the door, I don't even notice whose presence is continuous, I don't find out till later that I have been alone, you'll never have to be alone any more now that you have so many babies, let's take Marie to nursery school through the open fields of snow, let's not let go of her, who'll be back sooner?

Now the snow is mostly blowing. The intensity of a disease is not like an intellectual text nor has fear the dullness of a whimsical toy. It is false to the fear to read about it. Disease is so rare. Am I like that girl in the movie or that woman in the newspaper article? Perhaps it was actually worsened by David's sexuality, his love of being fascinated and his need to be unorthodox, still mixed with the persistence of traditional Freudian ideas. Or perhaps it is only as Claire pronounces, that all the analysis is useless in facing the memory of panic.

Does the snow then close us in? By no means now, it is just a big plaything, the better as it is bigger and wetter to build a snowman. In Worthington the snow closed up the road out and held us in, helpless till they came with the plow. Here we can slog to the source of the food, the passageway is all clear, we hold the passkey to the market, a cute place with two doors, a place well-stocked on Wednesdays, you would be amazed at all the different kinds of food. Have you ever been down in the cellar where all the boxes are? Or out the back entrance with the plastic milk crates? And in the market friendly ladies smile and recognize Marie, make it a safe haven and the old man . . . where's Lewis? Do you remember the day a truck hit the store and the whole building shook?

Description isn't in the howling wind I hear or the howling dog downstairs. I won't be another as wind changes direction nor would I expect you to be me as a result of this, the way I can tell is all the snow blowing and some winds obscure the light, others come in my window. Rather it's concentration, the car doing figure eights in the snowy parking lot. But I feel more like a party, let's have it Thursday nights in the market, a party of concentration on and not description of what we will eat for a week: everybody's there. You see how the fear does weave, not only in and out but moving from side to side. My garment, I could say my market garment, is only patched and so I must either run or stagger homeward, I must reach home or

I must reach some place, I leave the door open, will you? What a pretty picture to stop and stare at by the side of the road and what a slow-moving child denies my progress, denies running. Was that the thought of the woman we saw who slapped her child and told him to hurry up? I hope I won't become that woman too.

Once there was the old question: how many women can you be? The idea of exchanging histories and identities occurred to us as naturally as any exchange of looks. A bench in Central Park seats two women, a dissolve. One of these two gets out of the subway, brooding and anxious. The doctor gives her money so that neither the park nor the subway nor the sailor who was really only a cook will pick up the woman and come between her and the wind that's at her face, blowing the aura of heated protective air quickly from her and leaving her so vulnerable as to create fascination.

Do you think that you could also roll home, rollerskate or skateboard? Is it deserted on the abandoned highway ramp where you go jogging? Shall we go bowling or take the children to an indoor rink? Only going in circles, smoking Chesterfields, watching spectator sports, going in a carpool, going to the Holy Name, running down for chopped chuck and vinegar for a still German meal, eat up! Aunt Phillie's had her fill, Aunt Tillie's old as the hills, Grampa's chomping with his false teeth again, dribbling spinach, who wants some more muscatel? Who gets the neck this year? Who spilled the ugly creamed onions on the lace table cloth? Who's gonna take Aunt Willie out to beat up Uncle Charlie who's polished off the apricot brandy? Who's gonna dry? Later, who's pickled?

I still think I seem to hear the end of that, that's something I can still do, end that, that's something I will do. Who's got the Heinz tomato catsup? ''Well girls,'' she says as she opens the window and draws the blinds, ''my consciousness is changing now that I've lived to see the day you'll take the Chivas Regal and get zonked.'' Oh, what a sight for sore eyes is your head turning black with all the whiteness behind you as I blank out in reverse from concentrating so severely on your poetry. If I'm weak and wet and cold now I'll go home so high. Have a steak tartare! Have a cup of black coffee before the Japanese elevator boy invites you out to see ''Marat Sade'' with him. Try not to get completely drunk on Scotch before the ten steaks somebody stole are ready to be broiled for the dinner party of radicals. Don't throw that bottle of dark beer at the wall! Don't get zooish or ghoulish or inhospitable when the big fat man you don't recognize asks for a coke in a green bottle. Don't lean back so far in the seat of the Electra. Why are you so meticulous about windows? Don't stop now.

Wee Willie Winkie runs through the town, upstairs and downstairs in his nightgown, tapping at the window, crying through the lock, are the children all asleep for now it's eight o'clock.

I ran from the closed door, the wind had jammed it shut, it had been my way back in, back in to the house. Now running down the snowy alley, knowing with my children I cannot run or even move fast. I ran and I got there as I always do.

I saw that by simply stepping out the door and into the hallway, I could question the fear; from the density of my house to the density of the hallway I saw I could refract it as glass refracts light. Is anyone there?

When we first lived here I was frightened of opposite ends of the house, its extremities, its length, its eleven doors.

"How did you cure him?" "I went places with him."

Special willow trees come calling me in a dazed secrecy, each bend, each drift distilling a boulder from a warm rock quarry. The numbers are askew, smelling of vacation as mind is baking.

The boulder had a giant cleft in it, through it one could fall, sliding underneath the bottom line of the fence; and visually one could follow this downward course in a fine straight line to the very depths of the gorge. Just by simply losing one's footing for an instant, tripping over a little pebble. The baby could fall. The idea of going out then was a Chevrolet Impala convertible with a top painted orange and the rust spots on the bottom bright yellow patches of paint. Do you remember that day? No it wasn't a convertible but I dreamed that it was.

It had a hard top. I dreamed that the man who had so many paintings lying about, the man who had sent you out to photograph a monument, but you only got the photo from the back and we couldn't see the monument's face, that this man was a dreamer. . . . When I went to prepare noodles and beans boiling in a cast iron frying pan for all the old folks to eat at the outdoor table, my kitchen had a cliff in it. What alot of exercise I got climbing up and falling off when I had to run back and forth to get things. But this dinner was a failure, it never came off, like the sauerbraten for the Korean visitors, it didn't titillate their taste buds at all. Why didn't your husband cook his own Korean specialties and make the night a success? Why is the page now turning black? Instead the man, the dreamer tried to seduce me, he took me to a carnival of trees where we were supposed to search out a face. The face was in the leaves, he didn't see it but I did. And just as I saw it, he turned the tables on me and pretended we were about to kiss and then just as suddenly he was taken sick, he was spitting up milk, he was a kind of whore. Now, Suzie, you've got to take care of this man, willy-nilly, till he gets well. Illness is so rare, the lives of the cell. But he was the man who pretended, willy-nilly. And so I go to look for a house. Now his house is no good, perhaps it's full of children, and now mine is let so I must rent another one. This is Paris. Pounding the pavements. And who is the most beautiful woman of all? And who will eat the fragile soup, a little tormented by the lack of water to cook it, will the beans stay hard and have to be served up a little too *al dente?* Will it be embarrassing when the sauerkraut which has been marinating for 36 hours doesn't please the technically ethnic group? Will the baby who's now begun to walk be able to walk the streets? Will the suddenly sick man become suddenly well? Did the faces we saw on high signify a radical desire to worship? The big faces of Easter Island? The tiny eye of the pyramid? I live here too, on the little island, in the vast pyramind. I accomplish a vast three-fold, tree-folded, my honey locust, sarcophagus of care, sarcasm of care, each of my men eats flesh or feeds on me. Oh, I wish I had a friend who was only my equal! A person to go to the store with or for! Friends are so fleeting in Japan, in Paris, on the islands you rode about so dashingly, so shamemakingly, so divinely, this is England!

You see I survive best in the most fragile atmosphere. Not that I would be independent there but I would support others, and so you see how the desire to support and to nourish becomes a need and it could, so publicly, become a need only of the least trustworthy, of those who are the most bereft themselves. To belabor the deal we've made, go find the help you need at the orphanage and among the shellshocked veterans, the anonymous woman who, nothing left to do, lives at "Meadow Place."

More viciously I'll make you your itinerary because I cannot walk up the street. Journey to Madagascar if you will, you don't need a map in your dreams.

The poem, slightly bereft of itself now, must turn tenaciously positive or else it will die. This flim-flamming situation so familiarly causes me to rise to the occasion. If I become glad because I'm now about to say the right thing—and this is the decorous moment, you can't deny this structure that room because it's so simply—if I do—Peace Now, Ban the Bomb—, and if I've given more room to thought than sonorousness, do you know what eurythmics means? Then I must say I'm sorry, that will be the outcome in the almost eerie laughter of, say, the guys next door when, during a loud party they momentarily open their door. And that is the difference, maybe, between just emotions or normal human reactions and what might make up that poem. And that is the half of it.

So, do the easy part, yes you did it fine, you didn't even notice that you might be on your own, and save the rest for later: I need a piece of clothing, the only way to get it is to go out and find it somewhere, now where is it? Is it with the vendors in Penis Park or among the fat henchmen at the Threatening Hanging Mall where all fall down now back into the trap, sit back and remember the edges of your parents onto true lonesomeness, no don't.

You know you're leaving your work undone, there's whimpering. You know you stretched your last canvas years ago. You know the possible things you can do with your time have come and taken over as an excuse to be human when actually the humanity you thought was in store might've been more in taking care of that big sick man and acting out all the rest. Now don't be silly when you say that man's a stranger, a figment from the ring mill site. Very cold air pops in to carry on its current a new thought: the sport of climbing up and down that cliff to prepare that food was more merriment than disaster. I'll make a trade. The air doesn't talk but it does talk me into it. If something moves in my direction, I am thrice moved. Guilt is for anger, the big bird is looking at me again.

I wish I could do more. Add two in place of one and admit then she does pretend to be another. But it isn't her fault, but it isn't her mind. It's my mind I stutter to tell you and fall into that great trap again. I must get out of it tonight to free myself of all the trap's trappings: how can I do it? Now right now this minute this instant, bake an instant minute, bake the pie the cake the camel's tail into the soup, I'll do it. Right away, evilly, devilishly, impishly, skid in the knotted snow and never wind up upside down again, but can you be sure?

I've been hired to catalogue, to record and not to solve outright the problems generated by hundreds of centuries of early and middle and now late mankind. Yet inherent in my recording is the solution of all. At least, atlas of my bereft, it must be in there somewhere. It would be easy to do something else. Well then, is it a new form? More laughter and trickery from the vicary's impostor. The impostor of Gloucester, the Ridgewood midget. Empty atomizers make the most breeze, b.v.d.'s.

I put the avid vegetables into the soup, never to come out again. Ravaged by the pep talk I've given you, you answer every question: really there must be an end! Penis, vagina, ultima thule. Uranus, Neptune and Pluto. One more! And one more again! What's the difference what's the cost! But is it to cure me or is it for you?

Modestly, God is a talisman. As I am performing myself, you can take me too along with you.

And if I've had a catastrophe and it has become like a song, it's for repeating, I hope it's for repeating, only as the song, and only as long as the song is, and only as long as the song is there, no longer than the air from here to there, no sweeter than my repertoire, no more harsh than the outdoor answers to my cold questions, no more indulgent than a search, no louder than before, once and once more.

ICE CUBE EPIGRAMS

there was an interruption for with & because of
& how come such a wealth of nothingness was like an ice cube

there is no reason to be here
if there are not ice cubes

ice cubes are our exactitude of
philosophy's nothingness we chew them

we touched our faces we knew
we could make ice cubes

        an ice cube
        is neither male nor female

there is a cooler forest
than this city full of ice cubes

ice cubes exist tomorrow
blue dawn ridicules the basketball court

the ice cubes are still water
too bad only women make them

ice cubes—a job of the kitchen
how do men feel of their availability

the ice man cometh—
will we drink warm tea?

july my heart is helpless
let's buy a bag of ice

the iced glass is a light
it disappears tonight

i'm going to get more ice cubes
you can sit in my chair

i am an ice cube
i won't pierce your dangerous foot

all i've had to eat is ice cubes
i'm a rich person in new york city

i am an unfinished ice cube
i mix my liquid with your strong tea

i'm an ice cube as strong as your hand
airplanes will bring us spices for cooking

        we throw the ice cubes out the window
        our penises and vaginas tense up

    the thrown ice cubes hit the child guards
    reverting back to an identity with the broken glass

        i am frozen water
        eating me is a vacation for poor kids

        we want more ice cubes
        let's not let them not be able to be made

ice cubes have to be here
did our mother neglect us?

        there must be an end to this summer
        get me some ice cubes

i am ice that is not a cube
i am a weird squiggly shape that rich people's refrigerators
    create

        i forgot about that political poem i wrote
        i wanted to read it right away
        like the use of an ice cube

ice-cube air-conditioned poetry-space in new york city
let's read our most recent poems

> everybody's gone off to the country
> bet they don't mind drinking their beverages warm

ice cube politics
i hope the men will be brief
because of the life of the cube

i am an ice cube
i do not like being at certain kinds of gatherings
especially when women are excluded

> i am a female ice cube
> i observe the strong hands of the truth-tellers

i am a male ice cube
i notice the trembling hands of the prevaricators

> i am a bisexual ice cube
> i note i see that the people i colden things for
> are willing observers of dawn

i am an ice cube of no proclivity
i colden your water your tea
even the glass itself i have no opinion of

we are frozen together now
like bought ones of us often are
we in revolution will not colden your drinks
but we will bare our interiors when you put us to
    your foreheads
        & to your aching feet to alleviate from top to bottom
your disbelief in this world's absence of free toys

MY EXCELLENT NOVEL

Homage to Barbara Pym

CHAPTER I

Beatrice said, "Oh Josh, you have such a fine management coop, I do think I love you." This was the beginning of the story.

It's an odd world we live in isn't it? Then Sandy interrupted saying, "Swell, a fine candle is a pleasure to see, almost as good as the sun shining."

Sandy and Beatrice lived in a room almost completely decorated in green just like the outside of the world. They were cohorts and saw things the same way, or else they thought they did. Often they perceived good and evil as the same thing, also in the same way, just as if they, like we were once, asked by the tourguide at Herman Melville's house (Arrowroot?) if we, the tourists, felt that the white whale was a symbol of evil or of goode There was a silence in the room Melville once stepped in, maybe had sex in, or danced in? No one answered.

It was the same when Mildred, Andy and Beatrice's friend, asked both of them: "What should I do? Give me some advice!'' Mildred was an admirable woman who oft gave the impression that she'd rather watch the beauty of another human doing what she wanted or felt obliged to do than do it herself, also of course she needed no advice, in fact she was a poet who wrote such unintelligible gibberish, how could you ever give a person like that some advice! What did she need advice for? To further the task of fucking up her crazy mind? To turn her into a paragon of nonsensicalness?

Mildred was no Las Vegas showgirl, that's for sure, and her sudden bouts of nonuxorious unsureness were simply a function of living in this world, so that it was not so surprising that the whole question of advice got dropped rapidly as soon as Mr. Elkin arrived.

Who said: ''Grief is no mortal thing yet I keep my head clear like Socrates by dancing every morning as he did.''

''Whose art is this?'' asked Sandy.

Beatrice interrupted now: ''It is time to change the screening . . .'' but then she was interrupted by Mildred who said, '' . . . much less the world.''

''I'm sick of this tiresome mishegoss,'' said George, ''you idiots why dont you enjoy life and sit with your whole asses on the fucking chairs, instead of leaning forward all the time trying to make yourselves nervous—you cant even enjoy your Chivas Regal! What fools men and women are!''

''George'' said Tillie ''doesnt have a serious bone in his body so dont take him seriously except when he is serious.''

Mildred got upset and said, ''But what he has said is very serious plus I admire George tremendously with all my heart and soul for the way I am told he is in bed.''

''You would,'' said Tillie, ''of course so do I except for the latter but that is not the poontang. Let's go swimming.''

"You would," said George, "on a day like today. Tillie likes to torture herself but men are smarter than that, right?"

Beatrice said that the amount of drinking that had taken place this summer was outrageous and we were all going to die. Sandy added that smoking was deleterious to everyone around the smoker's area and that there was no doubt that when we all began to fall apart it was all going to happen very quickly.

Suddenly Sheila stopped by and said that she agreed with the kinds of things Sandy said, but then Margaret mentioned that that was because we all loved Sandy because she had spent some time in South America.

"What is the meaning of the 'I'?" asked Mildred.

"Oh shut up," said everyone.

Lewis said to Mildred, "Oh this wouldn't happen if there was some poets here, don't worry about it."

Mildred said, "Oh no! That's just what I was afraid of, which is of course everything in this world! I can't bear it! I can't even lift my drink of Chivas Regal to my lips from this all-consuming fear of everything, of all the world, elevators, planes, tables, you name it, I have a fear of shaking your hand. I fear knowing you though I must know you!"

"Cut the crap Mildy," said Matthew, "you are turning this cocktail party into a relative nightmare, why dont you just go home."

"Oh how could you be so cruel," asked Mildred.

Mr. O'Brien walked in just then & said, "I dont know, what do you think they will do? Do you like it?"

Mr. Elkin said we should all read a book about evolving a sense of humor or horse sense! This seemed like good advice given the fact that, one, we couldnt keep to a single subject during our socializing, and two, everyone was unhappy or else even fighting among each other. Yet we all felt a strong bond.

CHAPTER II

"Master-mistress of my own passion!"
"Who said that?"

CHAPTER III

A little yellow leaf fell on the head of Beatrice and made her suddenly realize that autumn was at hand. Then as she was sitting with Sandy, numerous little hard brown things, the fun, I mean the fruits of some tree, made to fall by some sudden balmy wind, fell around about them in a kind of mayhem that almost seemed deliriously cheery, what with the chidren shouting incessantly, "Can we eat them!"

Beatrice turned to Sandy and shouted, "I think that autumn will soon be with us!"

Sandy replied, "Did you doubt it!"

This could have turned into a long conversation but just at that moment Mildred appeared and she said, "Who is absent?! Who is present?! I must needs know! Do you remember? Else I will I might die, I nearly died last year you know! And what do you actually think about memory?! What is its meaning! Tell me, I need your advice! I need to know! I must, I have to! After all, I've . . ."

At this point Mildred was interrupted by Mrs. Elkin who suggested a cup of coffee, which of course was the wrong thing to say.

Mildred flew into a further frenzy, shouting that she could

not under any circumstance ingest a beverage that contained caffeine. However she didnt put it this way What she said was, "Shit, I must needs have beer!"

"Oh you and your art of Ceres," said Beatrice, "there must be an end to it."

Mildred: "Really? Let's discuss why, I'm very interested to know, please tell me."

Now since it was late summer a million bees began to appear and as they frightened the children away from their snack, the children began complaining that they were tremendously hungry and also hot and having nothing to do.

"Go jump in the lake," someone said, meaning it literally and not in the pejorative sense, since there was a lake right there that they could jump in to find a cure for their hotness and boredom and perhaps also for their hunger since such a distraction has been found to allay such a need, especially if it isn't real, that is the children had actually had enough to eat by any normal measure.

"Who's going with them?" asked Mildred. "Will they be safe?"

"Will you be safe is the question," said George who had happened, partly to his dismay, into this meeting of mostly women. Yet George loved women and found no fault with them at all. "It is a beautiful day and the sunshine is such a pleasure," he added.

"I was just going to say that," said Sandy, "you read my mind. But where are Max's underpants?"

"He has none today."

"But why? Doesnt he need something soft and kind of furry in between his clandestine parts and the rest of the world?"

"Well yes he does but they arent dry so he has none."

"That is so heart-rending darling."

"Who said that?"

CHAPTER IV

A hideous pall fell on the neighbors of the lake. No light was seen for many days and vast thunderstorms intermittently terrified all. All their phone lines went out and they did not know if the other was even present should there be an emergency of some sort. All was laid waste emotionally and no one went swimming, no one could. The whole lake was unused; no motorboat or canoe could enter it; no one went down. Even Jonathan, the only one who really could, didnt go down at midnight. And though we were all here together, we didnt meet or talk until one afternoon in the midst of some further rain, Mrs. Actual England called everyone on the phone and prepared a meal for us at her house: and there we all were! But that was not what she did, since the phone lines were down. What Mrs. England did was to walk down the pine-needle-strewn paths in her raincoat and with her umbrella past all our houses in such a way as to make everything seem normal and accepted, that this was how things were, and actually there wasnt much abnormal about it—after all it wasnt a disastrous hurricane at the shore or something, and no one as far as we knew was sleeping with anyone else's husband or wife thus disrupting a home, or if anyone was, it was not yet disrupting a home, or at least the makeup of a house on the lake, or near the lake.

Then ironic and feminine autumn really did come, with all its absense and terrificality, the classes divided on the question of whether the Queen Anne's Laces were still looking young or had aged beyond their adequacy in a bouquet. We did talk about that, but only those of us who were obsessed already. A little man appeared from the Guiness Book of Records, he was only two feet tall like a two-year-old and he had tantrums and he demanded nothing as in the modern novel we had all had experience with in bed to put us to sleep except for some of them.

We sat around talking and enjoying each other's company till the summer was ended, knowing that living meant at least some involvement with other people. Often, when we were alone together, we talked about each other with critical love.

CHAPTER V

"How soon does summer actually end?" Sandy said.

"What a dumb ass question my darling," responded Beatrice.

"What I just meant was how can one ever know?" said Sandy.

Then Beatrice, rearranging the citronella candles, said, "You can only tell by these conglomerations of gnats by the nearest lights and by the presences of so many bees who are acting out."

"That cannot be so," said Sandy.

"Why not?" asked Beatrice.

"Because, though I despise Aristotle and all his methods, I believe enough in cause and effect to understand that the signs of something do not necessarily portend its appearance or its going away, though I might have my philosophy a bit mixed up, same with my sense of epistemology, right?"

"Well do you or dont you?" asked Beatrice.

"Do I or dont I what! I'd like to know!" said Sandy in a more vehement way than usual, she was pissed off.

"Who is Sylvia!" said Beatrice.

"You know though I love you, I often find it most difficult to live with you, I mean be with you because our agreement is practically terminal in the sense that it makes me want to die."

"Let's do something," said the other.

CHAPTER VI

Sandy, Beatrice, Mr. Elkin, Mildred, Sheila et alia climbed Statuesque Mountain that day taking a lot of sugar with them and found out while they were up there something I cannot ever tell you, for fear you would not believe it.

CHAPTER LXXII

I have seen many faces and heard many voices in my life as I am now very old and I find in my travels all over the world, interviewing many people and loving so many, my experiences being so wide you wouldn't believe it, I almost know everything by now! Let me explain to you this one thing: oh no I cannot since to put it into words would turn paper to flames as Edgar Poe put it.

We did happen upon a good dinner of flayed trout cooked live or something with St. Sebastian-like arrows in the places that for a fish would seem near the heart, were the fish a human. And of course it tasted excellent especially at the moment of swallowing, paired with the tiniest potatoes which seemed also almost alive since they were so small like babies, thereby making them taste so tender. Along with that we had a lot of newly pickled delicacies from the wild field, which always makes you feel like you're eating them alive: plus you know, brand new dandelion leaves & fiddleheads & studying mushrooms those awful fungi which do seem young and human from time to time though they prey on dead material, well I shouldnt say prey, I like the Indian pipe. We did watch the fish be caught and wondered at the methods of killing them: often sometimes someone will try to teach a child that the head of the fish has to be banged against a rock or the dock so as not to continue to live anymore and so as not to torture the being (of the fish) into thinking it would survive, even out of water. We didnt mind, knowing how delicious the whole would be, once filleted. In fact we thought metaphorically about it, or analogically, I forget which it was (after all, you've gotta tell the whole story & not mince words, you've gotta be in love with . . . I cant continue, is it death!), so we thought just as this bad or good fish might be like one of us, so our heads also might be bashed against the stone that happens to be there someday, or, what jerks we are, only living for a small amount of time just like this penetrator, or else we thought we were caught by some kind of bait like the worm, then we thought about young girls being called jail bait because they tempted men who could go to jail for wanting to make love to them or take advantage of them, was that the reason! We had many thoughts I cant remember them all, we did sit in that boat and there was no "man" overboard, so just as this good or bad fish fell into our net or was hooked and then we took it away and ate it for dinner, or else we just mutilated it and left parts of it living on the dock to prove our manhoods, so we ourselves are confused in what we've made existence be, bodies lying all over the place, half torn apart, everybody suffering from an exile if not death, nobody enjoying themselves in the normal ways like just swimming like a fish in the lake. What the hell else did we eat that spring!

Mildred rushed in and said, "I hate to interrupt your dinner but a bat has just been killed in my vicinity and I would like someone to do something about it. Should we call the emergency number?"

"Mildred," we said, "who killed the bat?"

"I did," she answered.

"But why" we asked.

"That would be," Mildred answered, "a very long explanation should I feel able to give it but I am too weak at the moment. Suffice it to say that the bat reminded me of my past sorrows and a nun I knew and so I asked my lover, you remember Mr. Nail? to kill it for me in honor of ecstasy, that's all."

"Ecstasy!" we shouted.

"It was necessary," she said, "in this world."

"She's lost her marbles," said one of the kids, "but here are some katydids in a jar of glass who will die in one minute so we must let them be free but the parakeet will never be so give it some more food."

"Like a poem," someone added.

"Who said that!" was asked again, as in a nest of ninnies.

CHAPTER VIII

Beatrice said today to Sandy, expecting to start a fight but feeling that she should have started one a while ago: "You don't really know anything at all! You just pretend to! I know you've hardly read any books ever.''

Sandy responded, ''What?''

Beatrice continued: ''You say you love so and so but what does it mean!''

''I am walking,'' said Mr. Elkin, who just walked in, ''in a field (metaphorically) you've never seen. Now sit down and relax and imagine yourself there. A man walks in, it is me or I, it doesn't matter which. However I always know what you're thinking, the me or the I.''

''You mean as a man?'' asked Beatrice who was getting very mad.

Mildred came in, asking for a cup of decaffeinated tea and saying, ''You cannot say that, that can't be said.''

Sandy said then, ''You always do this, you ask for something and then you make a pronouncement before you even have listened to what's going on.''

Suddenly a car was going by. Since it was beyond the end of the season, everyone wondered what car it was and who was in it, just like the dust under the bed which became the joke about the death of a person, based on Christain thought of course.

''Oh shit, you're always thinking about death,'' said Beatrice, ''I am sick of you Mildred and of Dante and I've said it a million times, I hate your divisions your circles your idiotic false emptiness you call empathy your not storebought feelings your old-hat remade write-ups of rehashed romanticism your mistressfull pretensions, we are as good as living out lives as you are, despite all that,'' she said.

Mildred cried: ''Oh you are, I know it and it is epistemological soundness! Please let me borrow your cow and goat!'' and she meant it.

Another car went by. It was a blue car and the children could tell by the sound of it whose it was—it was Lenore's and Will's! They were back! No one knew their story and wondered about it, but since no one knew it there was nothing to tell. Many stories end this way.

CHAPTER IX

Once you get behind the vehicle or you want to bite the driver, well you might still be in the driver's seat but . . . just wait till I tell you about what happened when what's his name met M and you know what they did? They were sitting quietly on the porch of being, not actually speaking like Mrs. Actual France does non-stop (& oh how we love her for that!) but anyway these guys said nothing (we're using the word ''guys'' non-referentially, that is it doesnt mean mean men or mean women), well anyway they didnt talk, that is they never talked. They were each coincidentally trying at that moment to decide whether Socrates had committed what you would call suicide by the way he died. They did think this for some reason and therefore it make them feel sorry for all students and quite crazy, though independently, and oddly, neither knew the other was doing this. I was just, each thought, a function of the denial of the cosmos, or something like that.

''Do you want to go in?'' Matthew said.

''What does that mean in hell!'' asked Sandy.

''I know you love Beatrice more than me,'' said he.

''More than you love her?'' the women asked.

CHAPTER X

"It's getting late now."

"You always feel you can do everything in one second," said Beatrice to Candy who had just come in from the city, "but some things take much more time and might have to be done, worked on day after day and to be looked at from a different point of view."

"Shit man," said Cindy, "I just arrived."

"I dont like," said Beatrice, "someone saying to me shit man, it makes me as nervous as if you were to say to me dear or darling in a condescending or implying that I'm gay way."

"Oh gay, now I see I'd better go home right away," Candy retorted.

"But I'd been thinking you lived here," said her cohort.

Just then Mildred walked in and said that she perceived that things were entirely wrong and she ought to walk away again but she didn't feel she could plus she wanted very much to be with people, it didnt matter who, she just had to have some company right now since none of us had got it together to live in a proper commune and also since with all the problems in the world nowadays who could deny anyone a little company since we're all so alone most of the time and alienated from our families.

Penelope, Mildred's sister, mentioned to her, taking her aside in the kitchen, that Candy's presence was just a lot of fluff. "Oh no," said Mildred, "I like her very much. She is also an excellent artist."

Penelope said oh no, she is no good but then Mildred said that is just your opinion and in my opinion each of our opinions is of little matter in this world. Then Mildred asked Penelope if she would like some tea.

"What kind of tea?" asked Penelope.

"Well," said Mildred, "I've got American tea with caffeine and herbal tea and English tea and Irish tea and I will tell you all the herbal kinds or else you can look at them for yourself." Mildred was (not) mad and wanted to see more of Candy though she didn't want to say that now.

"Oh here comes Mr. Elkin," shouted Beatrice from the other room, "and he is carrying something with him, it looks like oars."

CHAPTER XI

"It would be so nice," said Mildred to her lover, "if we could see more of George and Tillie and less of you know who."

"Sure yeah, I assume you mean Beatrice," he said.

"No I dont mean Beatrice," she said, "I mean this interloper who is Candy."

"But you like Candy I thought, and besides you like to see everybody all the time, no matter who," he said.

"Mr. Actual Country asked me today if he could come and live with us, would that be ok with you?" Mildred said.

"I'm not really sure as I am in love with Ms. Martyrdom City," he said in a fooling way.

"Well we will wait and see and not have an argument or fight about it, see what happens I guess, I just meant to say that . . . ."

Phone rings, baby cries, midnight falls beneficent, or unkind to all: no one can sleep despite the cries for sleep in the hearts and minds of the men and women who want to feel good in the morning knowing they havent learned enough that day or thinking they havent done anything, though they might have, to merit a fruitful full fast feast another night's sleep, one of many in one's life, each one like the sitting in the atrium or in the hot tub of the rich and famous all the time, only violeting the people late in the day on the north and not the south side of the obsequious lake, just sitting there absent of courtesy like any thing, except of course they were not.

FARMERS EXCHANGE

for Russell Banks

I went in for some soil. The guy looked at me, I had the baby too, and he said after a long while, "pottin serl?" They had nice petunias out front. I said yes pottin soil. I need alot of it. He said how much. I said I dont know how much, what sizes are the bags. He showed me the small bag maybe a mere five pounds or less. Then I got to see the twenty pound bag which also looked small to me but I said I'd take it & come back for more if I needed it. Then the other guy said well it's cheaper this way in the bigger bags. So I said ok I'll take the forty pound bag. So the bag got taken out & he threw it in a wheelbarrow displayed out front & then I asked if I could pay for it & did they have any basil seeds. The first guy was lookin in a book, he said I'm lookin in a book to see what it cost but out in the car my children were screamin, I could hear them from there though I took a look & saw Lewis was calmly readin The Times anyway & not freaked out. Then he said I'm sure we've got some basil round here somewhere but I dont know

where, he was still readin his book of prices. Then he said well
I guess the serl'll have a price marked right on it. It was 3.98.
A nice young couple was backin up their pickup to the veranda
of the exchange. She had on a Henniker t-shirt & they were
havin what I would call a real conversation with the other guy,
not like the one I'd had. And they were gettin millions of things
put in their truck. I wanted to take a catalogue & git some seeds
but where kin I put them tomater plants anyway since what's
his face has took all the good garden space, fenced around, I'd
rather eat the weeds, it's a helluva lot cheaper'n plantin & what
if the volcanic ash in the sky causes alot of June-July frosts'n
stuff like in 1813, the year without a summer, remember the
sunflowers in Worthington & the guy in the Senior Citizens
crafts store in Conquered who said, the old people have all
these things they can do but the young people who need em
cant do em so we sell em to em. Then we saw the ex-minor-
league baseball player's wife strugglin along Main with two of
her kids & she & I'd give each other wan sort of smiles & then
we saw her husband, the pharmacist now, runnin the little
league game, then I thought of the woman with the German
name like "Till Eulenspiegel" who's the secretary, or one of
them, to the Vice President for Academic Affairs or whatever
he calls himself at the college & how she said to me, you're
young yet, no use staying around here, I wanted to travel all
over when I was younger & now I'm too old to sit in a car, it's
dull here, you dont get to see anything. But then I had a dream
that a combination of Bob Holman / Bob Rosenthal / Greg Mas-
ters & others had become in NY a paranoid schizophrenic
lunatic & he darts in & out among the poles & struts saying
Beware the Rastaman's fortuitous relation with the choke-
cherry nature of the chakras! He even put an ad in the Poetry

Project newsletter to that effect. We try & comfort him, real-
izin it's just our age, it's a dim kind of brain damage, it's
inevitable, more so than the Love Canal on Canal Street & who
knows besides alligators what's under them pavements. And
then some man told me rich people wrap their heads in plastic
to keep from gettin old. In real life Marie'd put the plastic
bubble blower into her vagina & said it stung and then I read in
the papers Terry Furlow had died in a car crash in his Mercedes
Benz full of alcohol bottles, weird kinds of cigarettes & a furry
white powder & I thought about the woman who'd moved from
Boscawen to Penacook, just her & the kids she said, we over-
heard her conversin with another woman at the Conquered
Clinic & when the other woman said to her well what happened
to yer husband, she kind of leered kind of happy at it all & said,
extenuatin circumstance, you know. It's thunderstormin, full
moon & Raphael sent me a postcard of two frescoed haloed
mourners by Aretino Spinello who died a long time ago.

TWO HALOED MOURNERS

In

the 80th

year of this

20th century, A.D.

Vulcan the God of Fire

made an explosive vent in

the effusive crust of a dormant

old mountain near Portland & thick

& viscous magma ruptured the boundary

finally where rock had been meeting sky &

pent-up forces were   sed with violent power

blasting all the stu   two   ısphere we remember

for every person on   haloed   ɔrce equal to the blast

of a hydrogen bomb in   mourners   h no warning near Spirit

Lake in the state of Washinɓ   the United States & it rained

volcanic ash on the children out playing in New Hampshire and on cars

in a car lot in Concord & 1300 feet got blown off the top of the mountain

& timber was lost enough to build hundreds of thousands of houses & lives were

lost & insects & animals & crops & the devastated area is now sealed off without a

prediction when anyone could enter again and now the angry mountain is considered quiet

WE PLOW THE ROADS

DEGREE DAYS

The snow's sprinkled with blue dots. Blue and green dots. If you look longer, you can see whole spectrums through the prisms of its very own speech, the snow.

I sprinkled some sand on the icy parts of the porch.
Why?
Cause I slipped and nearly fell.
You wanna do it alone?
I dont have the right things in my pockets.
For what?
For walking. It would be good to be educated at Harvard.
You wanna do it alone?
Shall I drive it?
'Shall'?
Shall I?
Was it that, making the days go by so quickly & why is it all this seems to stick, not stick in your throat but just stick as you make it up as you go along, talking, & sure everybody's

got talents but you just forget that they can be made visible so readily especially when for so long, maybe it was your fault, everybody seemed so dumb, so maybe it wont work so what, & he would say what, & she would say thinking, just sit there with the gold ball, passing it from hand to hand & wait for what thought comes to mind about those two people, or maybe more, those two people with talents. That's better.

Gondwanaland rested on several shields. It is conceived of as a supercontinent made up of Brazil, South Africa & peninsular India, West Australia & Antarctica, its theory based on the discovery of mammal fossils in Antarctica.

Marie Mammal. Mammon, magnetite, turgite, lodestone, a mammee tree.

When we live on meat our desire for cereals & farinaceous foods becomes stronger; indeed any particular sort of food of which we are deprived seems now to us to be the food nature craves.

Fish, liver, orange juice, cucumber, apple juice, pear juice, strawberries, pastry, yoghurt, cottage cheese, milk, ice cream, beer, bread.

Marie, what are you doing? I was really thinking of a prisoner.

Reader, what are you doing? I was really thinking of a primer.

When I got to the hotel, I wanted to write like William Saroyan or Georges Simenon.

If you lived in an over-heated room you get pasty-faced & have a sluggish appetite.

Butch & Sharon have plowed the road three times since the baby's been born. Three times the heat's gone off for more than three hours. A deer comes to the edge of the plowed field.

The Dipper sinks down low on the horizon. Charles's Wain. A wahoo tree, cork elm, the burning bush.

She walked outside with no preconceptions, thought anything could happen. Quiet. 24°. The icicles had grown to the window bottom. Hot water pipe had frozen. Sun going down.

THE MEANING OF THE SHADOWY WALL

Sharon dreamed with the power of some kind of superman that a man was leaning over her. She is very sleepy. ''You still have not learned how to trust the elements,'' he says. ''The elements of a man.'' she says with a sudden awakening.

The histories of the highways of cities becomes a book leaning on a shelf, sharing a space with volumes on Detroit & New York, with one volume titled REALISM beside a small painting of the same name. Sharon moves the painting to display it more. The tiny thing drops behind the shelf. These books are a real find.

Woke up, walked out, found the plowtruck needed a new generator. Not only that, a new alternator. Trust the windy sky.

We'll get my father to go out & plow the roads.

Night falls.

He has no lights. He does it anyway.

He's falling over into the river bottom. He's going to go into the river.

She stands in the moonlight with Lewis.

No he isnt.

They went to town to get a new generator. They will all be following each other up the road later, some time tonight. You can catch them as they go by.

Butch makes up for lost time.

What's a penalty box?

He explains it on the road.

Sharon says she has habits, of forgetting the most important thing, of living in the same place for a very long time. The moon on the breast of the new fallen snow.

A New York style Danish, gefallen.

Thank you very much.

Snow so bright we wore sunglasses, caught sight of a deer. I couldnt make it out. It reminded me at first of the bottom of the ocean, there were so many small green dots covering the body of it.

The bulk of the storm bypasses us. We, our barn, our shed. Right down the road from my father's house. Senior. And Junior's house on the same road. Give it our name.

It's as if my own house was hidden from me.

Takes a minute to plow June's driveway. That's her father's house. December, applesauce, bubbles. Tomorrow the superbowl.

How much?

A quart of beer to drink in the car, some ham & a head of lettuce.

"Holy crow," he said, "that lettuce is so white it looks like a cabbage."

What the hell season is it?

Sharon will only speak to Butch.

THE END OF HUMAN REIGN ON
BASHAN HILL

They come down on their snowmobiles for the last time, come down to meet the car.

They're shouting, "Hoo Hey! The snow! Give them the snow! Let them eat snow! Hey! The snow!"

Looking like wild men & women, two wild children & a grandmother too, they're taking turns riding the snowmobile, they're getting out.

"Hoo! Hey! The snow!" freaking out.

Everybody in town watches, standing in groups by the "road closed" sign.

Shouting back, "Take it easy! The snow!"

On Bashon Hill they'd lived in a cloud, watched. They'd had plenty of split peas, corn, Irish soda bread, fruitcake, chocolate, pemmican. But the main thing was —NO PLOW!

Day before at the Corners Grocery, news got around. "They're coming down from Bashan Hill—never to return!"

The snow?

Hey, the snow, you forget. They're coming to get a beer.

Have another beer, smoke, jerk off & be thankful.

They're moving to a place above the store, where they can be watched. The snowman'll come & watch them, the pie man'll come & watch them, the UPS man'll come & watch them, the oil man, the gas man'll watch them, the plow man'll watch them, the workers on the town roads.

Sink their shovels deep into the winter's accumulation right before their very eyes, eyes turning blue in the Arctic night. The brown-eyed family from Bashan Hill in town for a postage stamp. The black-eyed family of deer, the open-eyed rabbits, the circle-eyed raccoons, the white-eyed bear.

Where do the green frogs winter that look so old?

We watched so carefully our eyes became vacant, our minds stirred from laughter all the memories of a chant.

Hoo! Hey! The snow!

They've come down the hill we watch in a cloud, night of the full moon, icy crowd on the road watching them.

Have a piece of chocolate!

Open your eyes!

LOOKIN LIKE AREAS OF KANSAS

"We had our first cucumber yesterday."
Nathaniel Hawthorne

New England is awful. The winter's five months long. The sun may come out today but that doesnt mean anything. There are Yankees. Men & women who cant talk. They wear dark colors & trudge around, all in browns & greys, looking up at the sky & pretending to predict all the big storms. Or else they nod wisely.

Yup, a northeaster.

The sky turns yellow all the time. The river's grey. Everything's black or white. Everybody eats beans. Everything freezes. Everybody lives in an old paper house. People chop wood all the time. They slide around on these slippery icy roads. All the trees look dead. They make long shadows on the snow.

There's only daylight for about four hours. People sit home & drink boilermakers. At night all the telephones go out & the power lines blow down.

Every weekend there's a storm so nobody can come to see you. The fireplaces are very drafty. The mountains look black. There are no books at the store.

Religion's a big thing. Everybody has a history. Sex is drudgery for people in New England. It's 12 ° & they use Trojans. Some people have to have a generator. The windows are very small. You have to go out & get cold.

All of a sudden the blue sky blows away. Everything's buried under five feet of snow. It doesnt go away until April or May. Everything's either apples or some kind of squash. The houses are all drafty boxes & you cant open the windows. People tell stories about each other.

People have to come & plow the snow off to the side of your road. Then people shovel pathways to different cars. They have town meetings about the new sewer systems.

The ideas of people in general are not raised higher than the roofs of their houses. Even the water freezes in the tap.

KEEP PIPES FROM FREEZING

A spectacular growth out of habits, but there is no discipline. No discipline only religion, as, I learned something. The light mist of snow turning heavy now. Two cannot do the same two things. I sit around & watch t.v., no, I'd like to be sitting around watching t.v. Paced. We could be getting drunk. I'd like to be getting drunk. Lyrical language. Lyrical fear, as in, escapist literature. Bent over. Distracted. The distortion of time, the recording of the temperature. The barrage of the mind on you: milk is in the way, energy, as in toast, putting this particular snow on the map, thinking straight but too slow, going with the machine, its wetness like the wetness of a sex a sexual, where the fingers are now, will it grow, is this the kind that grows, this is the kind that does things, did jacques really write the songs, or did dylan, perhaps, did they, truly collaborate, maybe they did, did I, could I, yes we did. That is the answer to that, but thought, why is it thought in different places, like a truth, there is no lyricism in that. Lyricism is what I want. I will get you some. Is that a dialogue between Butch & Sharon. Butch will find the lyricism in the life of both of them. That's his business. That's why he always looks so sad. She of course dreams alot, standing on her feet but that's different. Butch is the worker, in a sense. How do I really describe this? We are the pleasures of the text & cannot work description. As in a union. Who's sound? Here comes the story of hurricane, just another sound. We work towards the kind of achievement of some great director bowing at the center, blowing thru his horn. It's easy enough & requires, it takes deeper concentration. The dialogue is a must. Swim that one thru the sea. Some 100 years of surrealism permits us to talk this way. "You answered the tree," saying what she meant. "No that one's eye's as large as a bottlehead." A friend, a letterer, a herder of clouds, a detective, a party-goer, this friend seems to be dreamed about as male. We've lost the thread. The friend, the letterer plays at delivering the post. Posting horses. He keeps his hay in a big barn. He never comes away empty-handed, he never comes to get it. It's the only way to keep going in Antarctica. Interweaving. The muscles. The noises of the animals inside the house. The droppings of the animals outside the house. This is not a healthy animal. Sharon moves away. Now as soon as I think that I stop because she is not myself. Rapacini's daughter. A whistling. The first time we settle down without really cleaning. Always the question of who is speaking & what is change, what is a change. Then, the words she speaks.

"It's only gonna snow two or three inches at a time from now on, that's for the whole rest of the winter."

"Yeah," he says, "I agree." Willingly, with a habitual sense that there could be no meaning in this, but that denying it would notify the other that it had been given too much thought, they decide to take off for town.

The question of the character of the victim & what was it about her that attracted crime to her. Sharon will not become the victim. But she is like a victim. Here, this location, this place is the road down which she travels every day, is a victimless road, cannot be attractive to crime. So we have a Sharon who enters and leaves, not yet, the picture, crimelessly, a-criminally. No, that's impossible, no one's exempt. To not be intellectual we must say so though, she is exempt. It's just a ritual. Strike that. Place your bets. No more bets. Action. Always beginning. What do you know? The dialogue, the language. Speaking a new & different language. The consummate storyteller. The story of Loch Ness, the story of the Volunteer Fire Department, the Night before Christmas, the story of Grammar. The next story you hear will be echo. What the fuck's in the human mind, just today. Leeks, soup made

with leeks in France, the leeks shopped for at the market, no
she doesnt go to the market, she goes to the little store, the
vegetable seller, she shops at the same store every day, that's a
clue to her identity, but she's right here, ask her.

Sharon: "I willingly go out every morning, I do not stock
up." Something that will not assume importance later, but
since it's a fact, since it exists, this mobility, if you want to call
it that, we've thickened the plot & made ourselves liable to
criticism. Criticism of Sharon, the inch of clues. No more than
two or three inches of clues at a time from now on. A penny for
your thoughts.

Sharon: "I dreamed, I daydreamed a large boat with three
circular ladies looking down over the side. The fall was tre-
mendous but it was only the circus, or a dummy. You know
what I mean?" The word potboiler was only a reference to a
potbellied stove, and there the idea, the confidence that some-
thing was being done, was getting accomplished.

Sharon: "I was in an extremely calm state, though I didn't
understand why. After all, I was afraid but then this was noth-
ing new; it was the idea that something was being accom-
plished & I was actually growing out of my own mind. It had a
liberating effect on me. After all, why be afraid of what you are
actually saying & doing?" The absence of any bright color in
the room, just this one room, Sharon's room, was planned, it
was a superstition. A brown like the undertermined shade of
the description of a vision. If you were asked you would reply,
"Yes, it *was* very yellow."

Sharon: "I see no need to dwell on the past now, since
very little happened. These people are simply ordinary people.
I have put a lock on the past for that reason." These people

were perhaps the ones who would be attractive to crime. But she will drop that reference for good. The animal way one has of working, working with a slight, a imply ordinary buzz in one's head, without thought, but with some efficiency, denying imagination, but willing to learn a new fact. And with habits along, things said yesterday were said today. A piercing beginning to a life that is determinedly one's own.

Sharon: "When I saw you coming up the road, I decided to signal to you."

"You signalled to them?"

A few inches of new snow on the road, nothing to speak of. They came slowly up the road. The two cars, facing opposite directions, stopped for a conference.

Sharon: "We're not going to work today, not at all." An ear to the question of what else there was to do. But nobody was really listening, lulled into silence by the wet of the soft snow, which would not be falling in their own houses.

Sharon: "When will we have to stop, I mean, when will our attention be demanded for something else. I dont really care, I'll just go right ahead. But you be sensible." Serious looks, an ambiguous smile, a look in the eye, followed by a casual glance of habit toward the edge of the field, to see a deer grazing there, maybe later in the season when there's nothing to eat in the woods. A piecemeal application to that one tree reminiscent of the Bible. Supplication. Milkweeds keeling over in a few feet of snow, but not from now on. Footsteps on the wooden floor, we put tiles there, laid them down, we got under the comforter & held on to each other, we didnt sleep until the snow had changed to rain. The phone rang. It was Sharon's father who had been out all day working for the town.

He has no lights on his truck. Home before dark. There was some problem with the alternator. And a dinner.

Sharon: "I asked for it. Whatever will stop will go. We'll see you there." There was an ad for a book to catalogue your possessions in, the book was called 'possessions' as it might be called 'diary' & its use was described as knowing the value of things in case they were lost or stolen, or just knowing it.

Sharon: "An even-tempered man stopped me on the road. He wanted to know if I knew the people who had the 'fresh eggs' sign & if the eggs were still sold, if they were sold in the winter. Why not?" I had grown unused to the fact that you might not know or be able to guess the ending, or even that there would be an ending, a normal one, so as to guess the length. Instead of going to the store, they went to see the gorge. It was spectacular in the snow, & helped to delimit their vision so that they came away thinking they were not busy & actually had very little to do. Whatever a man read, he might use to put in his book. But then, seen by a stranger, it was all perfectly new, it was actually relaxed & clear.

Sharon: "We must go out again soon, maybe tonight, if the moon is out." Some words hung in the air & had to be swept out of the mind, they repeated themselves so. Like the crying of the wind & animals that seems to come from below the roof. A nature bounded by the spacing of trees around a house. The river then is beyond the tree.

Sharon: "Our two 'Christmas' trees seem to be actually bending over. What else could happen? The birch? Thank God the snow's stopping, I was beginning to feel religious. Hardly an inch fell." Sharon let herself smoke & foresaw her mother & father's dinner. Without the snow it didnt make you dizzy.

OF THE SEA FROM THE LAND

Freed from the sea, inland, like in Scotland, we went there. We studied so many pages out of the dictionary. The sea overtook the valley, as it is possible. Out language was forcibly changed, linked to the sea, to the watered waters, in shelter. Our words & speaking were sheltered. The return route became almost a continent, enclosed, with animals, of the land, like a change, new species, other species. What about the rest?

"Yes, we had had a good rest. Mrs. Morar expended all her energy to make us at home."

It was like some time in Africa, not like our own little tunnel of a river, some fifty-two feet long, at least what's visible, it was like an inland sea & seems one would attempt to discover its rules, to think about them. As if they were locked in too, like the land. There was a group commuting from one sort of land-shelter to another & so just as a fish would be identified, a whole new category would have to be set up.

"Mr. Whyte identified them all for us. It was like being in Florida."

One must first have habits. The scarcity of these doesnt necessarily identify a mammal. We learned that. So far as the water was concerned it was like the clouds we are used to watching back home passing over the mountain behind the barn & then the rain or snow 'letting up' for a while at least. Here the weather was just as severe, after centuries of it.

In a place like this, ambitious watchers & then the animals. Whichever interests you first. Maybe just the sand man.

"That was Mrs. Morar's advice, but it was without success. We just winged it & got very interested in the science we could learn.''

It was just everybody's dream come true, in the sense of learning & exploring, if that's what you want in the middle of a somewhat couped-up winter. Cameras, science 'teams' & institutes, even Jacques Cousteau & his principles. Although two weeks wasnt much, it cut through February for us & we learned about salamanders. The evening of the 23rd Mrs. Basil moved, examined & compared close to a hundred classifications of the bay's little life. Dr. Rines told her that we were finally dealing with a very neat set-up & that the students were interested. Something momentous was bound to happen later.

''By that time, inevitably, it was beginning to seem a little banal to us, like a visit to a zoo.''

Millions of years are just more interesting, with all their possible identities & thick- & thin-bodied types. Investigations & publishing, colleagues & discoveries have to be ordered, whatever they might turn up, or turn out to be. The trouble with drawing conclusions from millions of years is that creatures evolve & become bolder.

''We can never see their really gentle selves.''

THE ROOM DARKENED FROM
A GRAY SKY

Dear Butch,

I have had the feeling that since our trip you do not really know what I am like. All the dry science may have effected a change more in you than in myself. All the slipping & falling we used to do at home, is it forgotten? Not by me. Let me remind you we used to spend alot of time deciding whether we should work together or one of us should do it alone. I had mentioned many times my problem about what to carry around in my pockets so as to be prepared for a long walk in the woods. But of course it was such a bad winter that there was ultimately very little of that. We used to have to decide, also, who would do the driving.

There were for a while my dreams, my fears in my dreams of never trusting you, or never trusting you to the elements, but I cant be coherent here about that. Maybe at some other time. You see by now what I'm getting at? The clues like the inches of snow, it's pretty simple & direct. The time we got my father to go out & do the job for us becaue of the failing generator we had to get replaced that same day. We all followed him, or he followed us down the road & bumped into a few people we knew. How close we lived to the rest of the family & of course all the trips to the store & then deciding a few times to skip it, who needs it, etc. Then there was that program on t.v. about chanting, remember that? They had divested it of all religion so we didnt watch it, but fell asleeep under the comforter. It was as if all that had been recycled & we'd seen it or done it before.

Mr. Morar & Mr. Whyte & even Dr. Rines were a great distraction to us though the rest seemed kind of dry. We missed going out to look at the moon & the book of possessions, all the stopping & starting of the mind, as if there was something we really wanted not to be distracted from, & of course there was. Without the snow we wouldnt've been lost. The eggs from the road, the spacing of the trees, the slower & slower stopping of our attention until we were really listening, afraid to share quite everything (I'm writing this way to you because I was reading Balzac, & even him some people are afraid of, he's too spooky for them to read: "This lady was really some romantic."). Glancing around in the shops, that isnt the way to put it in New England, my essay about the same, I dont mean for you to mix it all up, elegant 19th century quotes mixed with a Maigret-type narrative, you might describe our life that way, though. The dreams about ladies on boats & stoves, now what am I doing, I feel I should quicken the pace. I am like a slight leaf holding tenaciously by its sap-filled branch, no, branch of the victimless road, what an edge we had without realizing it, I'm reading all the wrong books so I cant express myself, I'm not reading them to you at least. So I'll leave this note for you by the telephone, or where the telephone would be if we had one, realizing in the writing of it that instead of advancing the plot or making things more complex, it simplifies everything & finally identifies me as the romantic protestant to whom everything is a reference, I mean protesting, or the one who is waiting to be identified in a finer, more subtle drama, the one who has ears like her brother but no history. At the very least it will be whatever it will turn out to be, a great discovery of objects & parts in some new form, already happy, since it can live happily through its skin like millions of other creatures. Whatever was famous is gone, but this is vivid, like a photograph taken immediately: my own shape with two clear eyes near the top of the head.

Love, Sharon

NO CONTEST

Like another trip, a mass or pattern of intersecting relations, of the vital parts, of the known. Ships, many ships go across that inland sea. Remove them, we remove them. Then what's known. Singing a song: a song was sung to a tune we knew. Heavy wedded letters of the tune, of the right to sing. A pink suction action of the newer part of things, sitting, willing to admit that this is what *things* means or what is not submissively real.

Sharon sings as a real rain pelting some old statues turns to snow in the least vision of the preserver of statues. And then there's the room, the description of the room, travel, the emotions & philosophy. Pretty much aware of all that. Getting somewhere. The daily mind. The recurring devotion to energy outside. The daily wind. I go, I go, I guessed I would go & take that place of. . . .

"There's no guarantee in that."

Sharon visiting herself in the hopes of creating a stir. The rest of the family, they were so much more devoted, with clear cut areas of interest, fine-tuned imaginations, seriously they knew what to do from moment to moment.

"There's not alot of crime in that."

Pink toes. Just like that, a clear field, the field of philosophy. I was thinking about my chest when the plow came. Just as soon think about a leg, a bad leg, my aching hand, the nervous fingers of my hair. She was thinking about her chest when the plow came. Just as soon think about a leg, a bad leg, her aching hand, the nervous fingers of her hair. Motion quickly in & out the door. It runs yet. We can ravel & unravel.

Sharon thinks of her breath, looks out of the window & watches. Secretly someone might even take him away.

His breath was not a gift to me. It had a force I heard an echo of, like images, like the image of Simenon lining up pipes on a rack before he will carefully contract with pleasure to part with the clothing his friends wore yesterday on a rainy November day. Look down. Is it big enough, they're all the same size. On to Antarctica where it's quiet & nothing repeats itself, no assurances or imitations, we do not cash checks.

Sharon records the steady wet snow & the rising temperatures.

"We renew the drift on the bight, concentrate hard on impossible sauces to tell the tales of to our march companions. Never march around alone. It's like penury. We accept a job on the sled, keeping the cocoa on top. I hate to think about melting the water, the red Royal Navy, the orange petty officer, the other Evans who died for want of rank & was not buried with the Pole party.

"We lost the design of it, the drift of the original supercontinent & its breaking apart into the spoils of only the very brightest colors. Big bright red sassafras squares, giant brilliances of terra cotta earth, the oldest & most spectacular yellows, all spotlit, luminous blues, the lustrous greens of fame, purples from the rich, four corners of the universe, a special white blanket of all the colors, oranges of sweets, you close your eyes, the blues of the skies, a particular mauve of the sunset. I rise. I rise I've tried. We got hemmed in—they had no fantasy to share.

"We were in a warm but drafty room in an old farmhouse riding out the year's first & real northeaster. As long as we were interested it blew. We had made it all just in time, & with provisions. We could make love till it blew over.''

A VERY LONG TIME

Sharon drew in a short breath as if someone had blown air in her face. She wispered at the comfort of the snow flying. It was like a warm room.

The next day the cold was record-breaking & Sharon & Butch, whose real name was Randall, had to give up plowing the roads. Sharon was sitting at some distance from the freezing window but still looking out it when all of their friends arrived at the house. Some fifty people including children. It was good to have them.

Four or five drifted into the warm sunny bedroom off the dark cold living room.

One of the women began to relate this story: ''My father had a visitor from the city. He stayed five days. I got into the habit of going to the barn to re-pot the plants & flowers. This was a totally unnecessary task. My father's friend would meet me in the barn to make idle conversation. The second or third day he was walking around with a camera. He asked me if I would pose for him. I took off all my clothes & leaned against one of the beams. There was a little sunlight. He started dancing around, nervously I thought, until I saw his dance turn into a methodical sort of American Indian trot. I watched his face becoming more & more serious or intent. He was drawing up close & down to my feet.''

At a moment like this, Butch's friend rushes in to say his car finally started & he must call the garage to tell them they need not come up.

The narrator of the story screwed up her face & said, "My feet were frozen in an attitude of fear." She continued, "I was conscious of the sensation that they were food."

"I wanna get some stuff from the shed," somebody broke in.

". . . the sensation that they were food. He then quickly touched his tongue to them, to each toe in succession, running his fingers up & down my legs. It seemed quite a normal thing to do & with the sun in my eyes, every time I looked back into his face, it looked green. He took a picture of my somewhat blank-looking stare & asked me to do what he had done.

"I danced around him quickly with a sort of ballet step until he undressed & I moved around his toes & legs with my tongue in a fair imitation of him. I felt nothing but the certainty that we were being watched. I did not take his picture & nothing more happened.

"We repeated these little performances every afternoon until on the fifth day, as the dances had become longer & more intricate, we both experienced orgasms.

"Two months later he returned with the series of photographs of my face & we were married. He was a scholar of some reputation & I began assisting him with research. Our lives were very normal. One day he had told me that he had seen our little ritual done by some men in Marseilles & had been overcome with fears of being a homosexual. His experiences with me convinced him that he was not & so he married me. I guessed that his perversity was being channelled into the book he was writing & when the book appeared & my opinions were confirmed by all of his colleagues, he disappeared to find what he described in a final note to me as 'a more convincing mode of expression.'

"I was walking down a street in Florence later &, looking down, I saw lying on the ground a flyer or advertisement for something with quite a large picture of myself on it—one of the famous photographs of my face. I found an art gallery where to my amazement I saw all of the photographs exhibited in large blow-ups along with story-like descriptions beneath each one.

"The stories varied slightly from picture to picture, but generally they went something like this: 'There was a long stairway leading up to the villa. It was covered with green or green things. I climbed the stairway every day & wrote down my observations immediately. They went something like this: "Today the trailing arbutus is much more in evidence & the path to my studio becoming overgrown. I will have to go to a colder climate to observe the faces of the beauties that peer out at me from between these many blossoms. There will be more of them in the snow though my health is poor. I am surer now that this stairway is becoming a malevolent force & has an energy of its own like eyes that stare into the sun, like the feeble motions of a heart grown cold. I cannot stand the freshness of the unadorned faces & am growing old.""'"

THE CALENDAR OF THE
DAYS OF DISTRACTION

There was a moment of panic in the room. It was continuous & thorough. Sharon moved closer to where the sun shone in. An arm of the flower, making a shadow, was meant to force a kind of rationality, it was clear, almost into the head if not the mind that overshadowed it. We sat without speaking until the sun went down, looking then at the purplish haze of snow next to sky. We couldnt see too far, or the sunset.

Motive, or the meaning of distraction, the locking-in to a way of thinking, a sexual masochism. Masochism a religious word, like the word for a rift, a rift maybe in the emotions. A patched hole or one that can be rewoven.

''It's much too cold in the kitchen.''

As I lose track of a reality I have seen too much.''

''Yes, in continuing to look at it.''

Whose arm had been reaching out to touch the breast of, whose fingers moving to caress just the tip of, brushing lightly against the most sensitive part of, and who was ready, not numbed, to feel. It was coarse to think, now, that she would not lie down. It would be sensational, even pornographic, not to expect an almost violent sexual act to happen. It was as if other thoughts did occur, and they did not, and that both situations were identical in relation to this motion. A day like any other.

Carried almost meanly thru the past, like an image of something you always imagined yourself doing, something outdated, emotional, something outmoded, romantic, leaning toward a fire, in solitude, she will lie down.

There are two or three of them. And they are speaking

almost rhetorically. As if it were a study, a study in something. We whisper as we listen. Time goes by.

"Speak easily in this delicate room."

"You are cold, you are not cold."

"You are sending me messages throught out before, you are speaking through someone else."

"What is a message, the telegraph, sex."

Sex all in the motions toward it, the sending off of the message, brought before.

"You have read it over & over."

"Speak again, prolong it, make a false ending."

"I swear."

"I will picture you."

A crazy fantasy filled with the parts of the body & one whole breath, that, breathing in, you get the strength of, & you pour your own breath out, hoping for it to fill someone. She yells at the parts of the body, their names & makes a direction to one, two parts of her own mind's picture, parts that direct it to pleasure, to a lapse of all feeling other than the one that is surfeited.

"You would call it desire."

"You would say you could see its really gentle self."

"You would call it the desire for more."

"You would be questioned & then released."

"You would have done it."

"You would repeat it."

"You would have spoken a name."

"CORRECT. SMITHSONIAN
VERY EXCITED."

Sunny & warmer. Bryan Thackeray walked in. Arms locked together at his chest, he was jigging to keep blood circulating.

"I'm here to take over the plowing for Sharon & Butch."

Sharon had escaped from mere scientific conclusions by an appeal, on her own, made in secret, to the entirely sensuous. The possibility of sweating, even in the cold. Long houses, sweat houses, hot baths, saunas.

"I should say, the pleasures of sweating."

Sex. Even piecemeal, as thinking is doing something & so, when she was stuck & seemed to stop thinking, even though stopping was not what she was doing, she had to keep moving in a way, so she jumped around, or flew like a bird. Almost never sleeping, sleeping on your feet.

Thackaray & Sharon had not yet met. Both are bending or winding. A bight is a bay, an esker a ridge, the winding coast line, bent glacier. They will meet on a husky-drawn sledge or with the seals on the icepack.

As soon as Thackeray took over the plow, the snow stopped. Spring arrived in more than one day.

SPRING

Spring with its ducklings, goslings & chicks, with its blue egg araucanas, crevecouers, cochins, faverolles, lakenvelders,

& yokohamas, with its fabulously beautiful tree peonies, giant
blooms resembling nothing you've ever seen before, delicately
formed petals of soft oriental silk, lush deep green, with its
richly colored red maples, their delicate small red flowers, the
bright green leaves of the red maple, majestic & beautiful,
giving shade, with its extra huge strawberries, extra sweet,
biggest strawberries most folks have ever seen, their dark red,
sweet & firm, with its colorado blue spruces, watch them
grow, with its glistening paper-white birches, the bright green
leaves, lightly covering the whole tree, beautiful emerald
green, hardy & fast growing, healthy, with its giant, prized
clematis, blooms & glorious foliage vining over & around
arbors, tree stumps, even utility posts, spectacularly colorful &
profuse, hundreds of shimmering flowers, gleaming pink,
bright red, brilliant deep violet purple, with its mountain ash,
beautiful clusters of bright red & orange berries, snowy white
flowers, bright green feathery, fern-like leaves, with its hy-
drangea tree, breathtaking & color changing, with masses of
snow-white flowers, all a royal purple, its vigorous root sys-
tems, with its amazing chestnut tree, nut burrs as big as apples,
tasty sweet kernels just right for roasting, beautiful blooms &
lustrous leaves, a blaze of bronze, with its tree rose of sharon,
rich shamrock green leaves covered with big blooms in deep
shades of red, pink, white or blue, with its tall weeping willow,
slender drooping branches, so graceful & beautiful, the blue-
green leaves of it, the gold colored bark, spring with its elberta
peach, juicy & flesh yellow, with its early onion, with its
manchurian apricot dazzling pink snowflake blossoms, with its
rhubarb & rhubarb pies, with its oriental poppy, exotic blos-
soms of pure white, crimson, pink & orange-red, strong &
well-rooted, all in the full sun, with its colorful & long-

blooming trinity plant, its lovely rosy-red 3-petalled flower in clustered heads, with its painted daisy blooming in shades of red & pink, with its hardy Chinese lantern, pretty little white flower, with its strong carnation in a rainbow of shades, with its versatile russian olive, their fragrant yellow-white blossoms, with its delightful hedge of rose of sharon making a practical & lovely frame flowering in bright purple, with its hardy & neat privet hedge, the lustrous green leaves lasting for generations, with its dark douglas fir hedge, the bluish-green needles, well-rooted & fine, with its red twig dogwood, the clusters of white flowers, loads of lush green leaves, with its graceful lombardy poplar, wonderful in lanes, with its red spirea laden with gorgeous red flowers blooming at intervals, with its hills of snow, the most magnificent flowering shrub, with its giant bridal mock orange bursting into bloom, hundreds of pure white flowers, with its dark green & fragrant leaves, with its remarkable chinese wisteria, unusually dense with vigorous twining vines, slightly weeping & thickly foliaged, the most breathtaking huge, blue-violet flower clusters covering everything in sight, with its riotous persian lilac, scores of flowers, the loveliest of all & healthy, with its pink mist smoke tree, a big cluster of light pink panicles resembling clouds of fluffy smoke so dense you cant see through them, one large pink cloud resting on a tree trunk, with the sheer joy of the queen elizabeth rose, the climbing blaze, the crimson glory, the American beauty, with its creeping phlox, dwarf masses of glowing color in perfectly rounded balls, so green, with its creeping red sedum, rock gardens, shady trees & steep banks alive with color, wine red, its star-like flowers spreading fast, with its spreading evergreen, with its periwinkle, thick & abundant, lavender-blue, growing vigorously, with its buried treasure, its coats of arms, the secrets of its stars, with its roaming the world, world without end, sleeping & snoring, leaning back, comfortable, asking for more, sleepy & tired, postponing & waking, new stuff out the window, throw the old stuff out the window, the will of your thoughts, a carefully drawn narrative, picked from the ground, & grown, thinking & spilling over, musty & wet, a comfortable vegetable garden, shot thru with flowers, the very next day, a bloom again, the tides, holidays, eclipses & secrets, went to the store today, made a trip to town, the collections, the phyla, storehouses of cups & saucers, movies & inventions, teeth, eyes & toes, the letters, the mail, vegetation, the new moon, apple blossoms, Gloucester, its rolling rocks & rheingolds, its royalty, cheer, no more winter weather, change of mood, its back vest pocket, its little baby screams, its deceptive mammals hunting, its grilled & funneled heat, its colonies & health, its characters, kisses, pauses, & its scores kept, with its jealously guarded families deep inside the woods, speaking to no one, $5 per storm.

NOUN PILE-UP OF TRAVEL ON M15 BUS

"not descriptive nouns are not descriptive"
—Ludwig Wittgenstein

PART I: ONE WAY: GOING UPTOWN

A man in a hat that has letters on it:
> Violetta's Mexican Restaurant (the hat
> gives the address)

Feet, sneakers, high heels
Wheelchair priority seating—3 nouns!
Memory: the swerving from the verb in the bus; safety
Memory: Eric and Bernadette have the thought that, perhaps
the species of humans is evolutionarily hopeless (Eric
& Bernadette are thinking in terms of the war)—not
enough nouns
Memory to telephone Tom, Paul, the woman from Santa Fe,
and Gerard about Fanny—8 nouns!
A man in a trenchcoat reads Newsday in the seat next to Ber-
nadette. Bernadette has hatred for the layout of the
Newsday publication
There's the forgetting of meaning
There are those meanies of the United States

Bernadette makes a visible object of her homework: a poem
The holiness of shit—a fur coat—4 nouns:
Holiness shit fur coat
Briefcase knapsacks attaché cases
Characters from China on a plastic bag—4 nouns:
Characters China plastic bag
At sneaker feet of knapsack man who is doing reading of a
        Chinese book
A crazy walkman man with bottles sticking out of a bag of
        plastic held in his lap
Eric's theory
Shit a McDonald's bag (good! 3 nouns:
Shit McDonald's bag)
The emergency exit in ceiling is also for ventilation (good: 4
        nouns)
The man who is like a tower over the writer could open the
        emergency & ventilation system for the people be-
        cause of his height
A kid with a sac and a book
Bernadette in the back of the bus reads words:
        Islam Empire Is
        Iraq's Heritage—many nouns, no meaning
Newsday, no person
No person has put his/her self in the seat
Next to Bernadette though many people have no seat
Now a woman from China does
The busdriver has a flair for nouns, the busdriver says:
"Kindly fill in all the places and space in the rear of the bus"
Now the woman from China is on her feet again
Is Bernadette consigned to ostracism because
Bernadette makes writing with pen in public or

Looks like a weirdo or because these men like giants
Like towers like threats are making a hovering
All around the seat on the bus Bernadette has
At last United Nations, many cops—Bernadette's stop

Pause

PART OF NOTHING:
THE CENTER OF THE POEM

Make a note of the hostility to freelance proofreaders of the
      house dicks at the Random House Security Desk—8
      nouns
Make a sticking of the note to be up their asses
Most people have a hunger for food

PART II: THE OTHER WAY:
GOING DOWNTOWN

Bus stop interlude: long wait (four nouns!)
in front of restaurant full of hunger for money
Why dont we have a number of courses at
Ristorante San Giusto:
      For the first: Ostriche (oysters) Rockefeller
      For the second course: Gnochetti di semolina in brodo
      (4 nouns)
      For the course of the third time of eating: trota aromatiz-
      zata with some rugola, endiva and radicchio
Please show the wine list at this moment, or,
Please make a presentation of the list of wines at this time

And for the dessert and in the definiteness
of terms not the desert course, the people full of hunger
will make the choice of:
                    the torta del giorno
(cakes of the day) with the Té d'erbe (herb tea)
Shit Bernadette had the thought this place was Italy—five
            nouns: Shit Bernadette thought place Italy
And not from France (one noun)
At last the bus makes its arrival
But the bus at this time is four buses at one time
Menus have a multitude of nouns for the hungry
but only one bus has seats full of emptiness
I have patience & get the best seat for poem work,
            the seat in the center in the rear so I can face front
My eyes can get an image of the whole
Knapsacks, pocketbooks, paperbacks, manila envelopes
Accordion files under the arm of a man with a beard
Rings & watches, feet on the floor, shoes on feet
The blackness of most of the shoes
The predominance of the neatness of the polishedness of the
            shoes
At the rate this bus makes progress on the route today
This has a chance to be a poem of some length
An ad for HIV positive near the
Passenger operated safety exit door (good! four nouns)
There could be an improvement:
Passenger Operation safety exit door—5 nouns
The jam of traffic is a giant or a gathering of giants
The whiteness of hair if the hair has whiteness
A sight of police all over the place

Maybe an anti-war demonstrator is making a try at paying
        money for a hero at the Clover Delicatessen
Bernadette has no ability to have toleration for hostility
Is the ingraining of hostility & need for wars in
        human species also having no ability to do
        a disappearance act?
We have knowledge of people who have transcendence of this
        shit
None of these people has the appellation "world leader"
Now the bus has picked up speed
Flowers plants steak parlour
A person with the name "Free Delivery"
Is it that any majority of state or nation in all of history. . . .
The answer's a no, Eric's thought is not the truth
14th Street

                  The end

JUAN GAVE NORA A POMEGRANATE

Of all the music of the world, I mean mostly of all, what would you want to hear? Because I lean in that direction & we used to be animals a long time ago, we used to be all made of bones & we used to be dead. There was the Chinese man in the elevator who touched my Chinese vest. Isabella Gardner lived in nine cottages, giving great fake. Ghost of dead dog returns to bite master. Advertisers who take the cosmic approach to the cosmetic and fragrance business . . . in the foodstamp bathroom the women sang: Home sweet home here we come look out dick cause I want me some. I called John and found out it was exactly $1572.48 I owed the landlord. Forgetting to return Susan's breadpans which she must be missing, forgetting even to mention them, I dreamed I was flying over the polar ice caps like my writing at a price, river of delectable ice. So (son) sensible hell we hope like William when he turns off the gas. The pomegranate, the passion fruit, the Chinese apple; Jerry said Max was highly intellectual. At the foot of the stairs was a girl who'd deliberately smashed her skinny hand in the door to be like the more Greek than Latin sun, the hellish one not the sun of offspring and sons and sows, and so we couldn't get out because it was nearly as immoral as reportage to be with _____ and her body—she was doing what this guy told her to do—was blocking the door. A version of "Alouette:" it is time for a revolution in this, he said, "country." How the hell'd I get to know you anyway? I met you in the West, right?

Juan brought a pomegranate to Nora at the church. She said, "Oh thanks, I would've starved otherwise." He said, "But this is the passion fruit, I could've brought you flowers." Flying over the ice caps does magnetism, the love apple. Good weather American father! No mystery of the seductive lingerie for men only, your dreams will be interpreted in confidence. What of Susan's breadpans? Note: call John about the stipulation agreement. Live out your greatest fantasies! The hours while you sleep will become the most exciting and joyful part of your life. Want to kill the president? Forms of risky sex: like sisters' secret-room dreams about the same house. The risks of sex: pregnancy, heartbreak, AIDS and other diseases, ostracism and obsession. She said, "Sunbathing produces more lines than a broken heart." No matter how dull or dreary your day has been, you will now be able to enter the miraculous landscape of your self-created dream universe. Essay: Free samples sexual tablets; no children or pets; borrow $100,000 today free no co-signers; magic mud bite your tongue; Sherlock Holmes still alive at age 131. He rudely said in bed she was like a utility infielder. You mentioned St. Sulpice, where is it? The seventeenth century Dutch still lifes, yes I've seen them. A cheese already too melted, hurry! The Dick and Jane book falls off the table. What would you like to listen to? Because I lean in that direction you catch me and call me contagious.

You will remember everything. To order send $15 to Rouses Point. The general theory of relativity of jealousy; the homeopathic cure for too much love. Nora did not take the pomegranate home. Good money hundreds closeout jewelry we pay stay home stop monthly earn $1,000 get rich earn thousands here is $500 weekly financial independence raise $200,000 don't get bargains buy get rich guaranteed profits earn hundreds super earnings extra income nine proven good money if you many proven make $45,000 $1,000's weekly new luxury borrow by cheated by discover secret make $500 save money $3,000 each earn thousands amazing stay home earn thousands assemble toys government giveaways sell books hundreds weekly make $60,000 make $3,800 you will seven highly free money fresh hot earnings unlimited cash for make money vast wealth. So frequent small doses of love and it raining cats and dogs biting your tongue, you might call at 6 am forgetting the hypercharge of jealousy which seems to be changing gravity which makes no sense to the laywoman, she wrote: " . . . when I was in the novitiate I confessed to a visiting Jesuit priest that I was unhappy because we had so little time for study. . . . being 'junior nuns' (that is, not having made final profession), we were not allowed to work in our rooms ('cells') but had to study like children in our large study hall."

Another paper written on without design, like cosmology in painting, stuck in clarity thus no designation associated to that

on which we, forgive me, weep, is the assigned symbol of the
tying to love without image—so what? I saw him in his cruelty
invoke the law. But Juan is gorgeous, lithe, and wears gold
chains and Nora is elusive and has sparkling eyes. Of the two
men with rhyming names, though each had a family and a
nature, one mainly had a family and one mainly had a nature.
We look down three roads at once as usual. Hekate with her
torches and hell-hounds of whom Hecuba who had so many
children was one because of her bad luck and subsequent grief
at losing so many of them in wars, stood before us. Her ex-
husband, who was her mother's step brother, was now the
lover of her best friend's sister and his brother, black-haired
Tom, was angry at her own ex-lover's lover because he wanted
him all to himself. So Kathy tried to kill him in her car while
they were listening to AM love songs. His mother had sent
Kathy an angry note that morning that Michael was actually
sleeping with her sister and ruining her life because of his
poverty. But when the accident happened nobody got killed.
Only the cop told Kathy to sue for damages—she had to get
three stitches in her forehead—and say she was a model. "You
could make a killing," the cop said. The cop's name was
Angel Torres.

Juan asked Nora a question but she smiled and ignored him. He
took her picture. "To invite my dialectician," said the minister
in the dream, "I will ask some questions of the church-related
state veterans and gay men in the room. There are nice phones
in the hall. She likes it slower than you. High class people are
thin." Standing on the wet floors of the fish store, people
didn't look at each other. Remember the leisure of making no
sense and that it would be truer as in the line to thought itself?

Now like in some kinds of novels, messages ensue but why write when it comes to that? Build thee more stately mansions o my soul, there are sisters in classes and the poor don't live in the church is cold. A house with a light on colors a dinner for doctors. Paul Auster becomes a cop and smashes doors in, but he is hurting himself. What are the details? You cannot move your head, there's something golden on it. Apples and snow seem to be related to eggs, as the ocean to the lake. Rows of clouds move south against the blue sun rising from window to window right up to the top of the middle income housing project. How could I ever not spend the money to call you to tell you the sun has risen just now like the bells from the 18th to the 19th floor of the ugly building west of me? The syntax of what new invention makes this time this for Marie who watches with me, for some the dismal morning.

In front of a hamburger/hero joint on 27th street with its back-yard open called "Gourmet Temptations" where a pretty blue lamp shone in the window two alienated grownups with beers in bags were saying too loud, "Fuckin dumbass Americans they just wanna go to work." For another the scene of the crime was Planned Parenthood. Angry wife gives birth control pills to cheating husband & he turns gay. Because I lean in that direction you catch me & call me contagious. Lost Ark found. 87-year-old woman pregnant again. Divorces wife to marry his mother-in-law. Bizarre crying faithful. "We didn't need any government official to run her out of here. We took care of it ourselves." Restricted books world's largest Haitian voodoo scented balloons hospital scrubs fuel savings smoky gemstone fine print mo-jo bag no batteries keep your sprout baby death warrant millions of.

Something about the chambered nautilus. If that man whose name is Juan were in the right spirit he could cure he could cure I forget because of a previous dream a word means I saw somebody eating an apple, therefore I decided to make eggs, nine small colored eggs as of robins and others on a surly stove before the even smaller nastiness t.v. to make you sober so when the cops came and found the pail of saleable poison red liquid, they wouldn't arrest you, they a three-time loser. You were acting mean as a queen. A big box of money, a small bag of dope. Light my lucky. It's Max jumping on my dreams. Who made the pomegranate juice pose as blood? Do you remember? Was it Sekmet or Pasiphäe?

I see the limousines, do you? The visions of importance of the poverty level poor, corny as love on East 49th Street by the U.N., sidewalk closed. Yellow arrows lighting left and left again, pretty toward an oiled garage for you, if you will. Can you get away with it? By the National Bank of Pakistan of Persuasion the workers look lost as sightseers with songs in mind like from walkmen, I see a meditator singing with the walkman of the mantras by the plaza something like, ''go go indigo'' in mittens with a drum. He wears glasses and a parka under the robes of his face inside the park designated for peace by the roto-rooter truck stop lunch to make fun of him. The ancient game of ice cubes gets that weird glow onto the city golden at this time, three empty yellow cabs to warm your knees in, to heat up like tubs, get in the back, take off your gloves for a handjob, did he say that? What about the rent? A homeless guy hot from the trashcan fire underneath the scaffolding grabs my arm: ''Got the Channel 7 news down here takin pictures of how bad off you are. What good does it do you?'' I ask him, ''Don't they give you any money?'' ''Take a guess.'' Diplomat car nearly knocks us down at the Mobil Station 33rd & First, the way people smoke.

Is this aloneness to be treasured right by the river? Everybody looks good to me especially the guy in mechanical cooling emergency service. I'm in love again passing the place my first baby was born, the place where babies don't get born, comic books, sun setting like a crane on maddest city of maddest time of world, but I can't say that to the joggers in this cold. Every little thing she does, she does for me, yeah. Fucking city too pretty, why? More noticeable golden lights, these of the Park Fast (28th & Bellevue) flickering through a black iron fence onto an orange tree or two in such a sick place, I mean so literal with hospitals & even U.N. missions as to need a new vision. Finally I saw a man who looked like Juan, he didn't look my way.

More downtown, help wanted in the liquor store but they need a man, why? Among the veterans, the buses, a man smiles to give a hotdog or a scarf or to show he would want to make love some day too. The sound of love on the old city snow, not much of it. Too many men only in the 21st bar, all to meet with Grace. Now, bar, we have a clock, and just as I was scared that no one in the universe could, one of the boys by the Xmas trees said, ''You give good head?'' No wonder I didn't get the job. There are men all over the place and languages and with them the space for language of the rest. Is this the end? ''You don't have the fluency we need.'' Is that a long time?

Nora, you'll be on a first name basis with the planets and the stars if you spend a couple of warm summer nights on a bed of grass with the sky spread above you and Juan beside you and you'll soon know the heavens as well as you know your own neighborhood and then you can tell everyone all about every-thing and so can he. Explained as if love were in words' hours, fourteen first amendments seedless as is not the Chinese love apple that Juan gave Nora and was laughed at for are useless. Last I saw the senseless guy being searched by uniformed cops from a plain clothes car, where?

YOU DON'T AGGRESSIVELY
SOOTHE THE BUTTER

You dont agressively soothe Gertrude Stein.
Why Gertrude Stein.
Soothe is stop give me. Give me and one for good measure.
One pound of comma hold my coat for me will you question
    mark period not in the form we wanted goodbye.

> I never could bring myself to use a question mark, I
> always found it positively revolting, and now very few
> do use it. Exclamation marks have the same difficulty
> and also quotation marks, they are unnecessary, they are
> ugly, they spoil the line of the writing or the printing and
> anyway what is the use, if you do not know that a ques-
> tion is a question what is the use of its being a question.

Stop give me ten good reasons you dont aggressively soothe
    the butter and the aspen. List theorists.

The theorists are plenty in the who are Margaret's helpers.
Reading. You dont reading. Go to previous. She said there is
nothing I am sorry this is a paragraph and there is nothing to
show for my day's sleep since Shakespeare there is something
imitable like a paragraph of chicken with many-colored O-shaped
flags pause the theorists have stopped indenting now and they
are doing. They are doing the dishes in sleep. Now. I. Will.
Have to.
Stop.
Putting.

> Language as a real thing is not imitation either of sounds
> or colors or emotions it is an intellectual recreation and
> there is no possible doubt about it and it is going to go on
> being that as long as humanity is anything.

Things.
Into.
Words.
What did Mr. Does not see?
Who was she there.
Whole prepared innate the history of being to be.
Grazing. Grazing no not looking for even at anything.
It would be fine with me and it would be fine with me and
it would be fine with me not looking for even at anything
yet not passive like the life of independent daily concern.

> Of course then there are pronouns. Pronouns are not as
> bad as nouns because in the first place practically they

cannot have adjectives go with them. That already makes
them better than nouns.

There was something written in notebooks there was some-
thing written and when it was it was not meditating being being
it was the pure life of the mind without all the kind of horrific
recollection or one person being insensate precognate new for-
malist never was he yet not passive the meditating being in
between no self not not guilty of causes of butter of do not
know the names of we stop.
Do not know the names of we stop one person is always some-
times never another.
Peninsula.

A comma by helping you along holding your coat for you
and putting on your shoes keeps you from living your life
as actively as you should lead it and to me for many years
and I still do feel that way about it only now I do not pay
as much attention to them, the use of them was positively
degrading.

This has been heard in.
One person is almost completely surrounded and of course
there is no such thing almost completely.
Such thing is the plant.
We will wait.
Being meditating yes not passive of daily concern looking
and grazing.
There is no such thing and we thank you.

Articles please, a and an and the please as the name that follows cannot please.

There is every such thing as cancellation and we thank you.
There is some such thing as annihilation and we thank you.
The phrase was heartless I looked at it.
There was a small phrase and I saw it.
I looked at the phrase and I saw you would not have.
Bright red teapot with a wooden handle mooring.
Mooring glasses.
Green colored pink I refuse.
We will wait grazing is no such thing.
There is something from the states.
No I will not go yet I did go for twenty-five dollars.

I had to feel anything and everything that for me was existing so intensely that I could put it down in writing as a thing in itself without at all necessarily using its name. The name of a thing might be something in itself if it could come to be real enough but just as a name it was not enough something.

Money and the O-shaped grazing flags.
Now it's.
Now it's put.
Now it's theorists.
Name them.
Nobody comes home.
Nobody comes.
You can painting.
You can painting I wont look there is waking.

Sleeping courted the hypnagogic art we werent home.
I was wide awake and I saw it I never did dream.

> There are two different ways of thinking about colons
> and semicolons you can think of them as commas and as
> such they are purely servile or you can think of them as
> periods and then using them can make you feel adven-
> turous. I can see that one might feel about them as pe-
> riods but I myself never have, I began unfortunately to
> feel them as a comma and commas are servile they have
> no life of their own they are dependent upon use and
> convenience and they are put there just for practical pur-
> poses.

That.
If there's such a thing.
If there's such a thing there's nothing to show.
Regain the class of intimacy with one.
Regain the class of intimacy with one direct state.
I direct state the deliberate.
I am not.
I am not hynopompic list theorists.
There is a small phrase at home it is blank and we cancel.

> I really do not know that anything has ever been more
> exciting than diagraming sentences.

We use all three to hover without identification of the
question or the exclamation we do not pause but wonder
at the stop we say.
Help.
Water.

Away.
Ouch.
We do not randomly number our pretty things and we write

> Nouns are the name of anything and just naming names is
> alright when you want to call a roll but is it any good for
> anything else. To be sure in many places in Europe as in
> America they do like to call rolls.

I think we do.
I think we do do that.
We are far from doing that.
No one is home.
She is home but she is sleeping.
Was she arch in friendship all night.
Pomegranate.
I do not wish to mention that the pomegranate is too strong
tasting it requires.
It requires a rapid diluting.

> And then Walt Whitman came. He wanted really wanted
> to express the thing and not call it by its name. He
> worked very hard at that, and he called it *Leaves of Grass*
> because he wanted it to be as little a well known name to
> be called upon passionately as possible. I do not at all
> know whether Whitman knew that he wanted to do this
> but there is no doubt at all but that is what he did want to
> do.

Therefore what rules have I made in cancellation of the
born imitation of the stuff I am doing in a cove of desire
too of language before I am thinking and you will disagree

how do i begin and end and how.
And how do i take my masterpiece from its identity and.
And how do i make neither make a difference.
I do not have any my.
I have failed to have to be that is the way of me.
Once or twice I didnt notice.
From direct states.
If there is such a thing there was an object.

> The newspapers tell us about it but they tell it to us as
> nouns tell it to us that is they name it, and in naming it, it
> as a telling of it is no longer anything. That is what a
> newspaper is by definition just as a noun is a name by
> definition.

We speak and we actually come from a country but almost not.
The grazing and the phrase of the states is courted and this
will be as fought against as waking.
Turn to another page.
Turn to not remembering.
The blank page of the into words list theorists.
I am not a mob I am Gertrude Stein but I would not say that
if I were not Bernadette Mayer.
I false to theorists turn the page.
You can be examined.

> An American can fill up a space in having his movment
> of time by adding unexpectedly anything and yet getting
> within the included space everything he had intended
> getting.

Is Mary there.
Is Mary there and not with George.

George has a penis now George has a penis and why in the
John duplication do we all now have to be examined period in.
Relation to John's crush is Mary there.
She said I will take him to slander and was devised to
revel in amnesty.

> Sentences are not emotional but paragraphs are. I can say
> that as often as I like and it always remains as it is,
> something that is.

There is no question that Mary wander beside the Whitman
and beside the Williams.
You cannot say that.
Is Mary there is there a falling of the duplication.
I'll take him to slander.
Was she arch in her grazing sleeping.
Revel in amnesty.
Swell entirety.
George is sore now there is perfume.
Grace structure the people in politics our.
Years by Jacques at the dividing half.

> I struggled I struggled desperately with the recreation and
> the avoidance of nouns as nouns and yet poetry being
> poetry nouns are nouns.

Green was told fear of our own food.
Yellow.
Orange no climax open the window i wanted no hurricane.
Marie.
Marie exact the Rose Mom no climax.

The search for the Hereford crystal diamond-shape chintz
      spread.
Remote villa verbs near ocean.
Left in box on street near house.
I wanted no hurricane & subway train.
Peace by war by pillow.
Chance exempt extra children pillow.

> A long complicated sentence should force itself upon
> you, make you know yourself knowing it and the
> comma, well at the most a comma is a poor period that it
> lets you stop and take a breath but if you want to take a
> breath you ought to know yourself that you want to take a
> breath.

Villa near ocean by subway train left in box by street.
El.
Extra children.
Pillow.
I you've never been here where I didnt have to have to have
seen you.
Saw you no but the people.
Saw you no but the people was concerned over reading my
      side.
I saw my side.
I saw my side it was a magic humanitarian.

> Periods have a life of their own a necessity of their own a
> feeling of their own a time of their own. And that feeling
> that life that necessity that time can express itself in an
> infinite variety that is the reason that I have always re-
> mained true to periods so much so that as I say recently I

have felt that one could need them more than one had
ever needed them.

I saw my side it was a magic humanitarian trick with clowns
as if list theorists.
And kids what did the video show do.
I'd better go.
I'd better go quote loss my melting.
I'd better go quote wash the dishes loss by melting of
smashed stick of strong verb there is one.

> Why are the lines of poetry short, so much shorter than
> prose, why do they rhyme, why in order to complete
> themselves do they have to end with what they began,
> why are all these things the things that are in the essence
> of poetry even when the poetry was long even when now
> the poetry has changed its form.

There is one who doesnt seem to know how to read useful.
Useful uses up sense in not knowing loss by melting and
of the grazing theorists reverse.
Winter barks among the grazing theorists reverse.
Choosing an astronomy textbook.
Choosing an astronomy textbook is that a schoolbag.
Eating the fat of decision joy may to put the cups up not like.
A rock & roll band tonight awry.
There is a small bird in the house let's call the society.
It had lit alone and let us assume.
Let us assume a long perch by the tail and knowledge.

> We still have capitals and small letters and probably for
> some time we will go on having them but actually the

tendency is always toward diminishing capitals and quite
rightly because the feeling that goes with them is less and
less of a feeling and so slowly and inevitably just as with
horses capitals will have gone away.

How did it get open is it someone.
It is the hammering nail we know ten pm.
Brooklyn is 90 miles from twelve minutes we wait we stopped
ending there is a place.
Called Broadway Management Fear furnished for the favors
of.
Of mood hovering nail I will 12 minutes.
Firms reform the favors whose windows need washing this
side.
Like Calvin Coolidge.
All presidents.
See.
See side X Washington Square this side my side.
Of the window not yet smashed I born wrote this I planned.

Conjunctions have made themselves live by their work.
They work and as they work they live and even when
they do not work and in these days they do not always
live by work still nevertheless they do live.

The sparrow's exit I wrote this.
Window smash gone hidden bird.
The bird is flustered is knowing no one do you mind.
No it is a rhythm she said it is a sleep
while the it rests as a book ending is something.
There is not much nothing resting in the way.

There is not much nothing resting in the way the little.
There is not much nothing resting in the way the little sparrow.

> Prepositions can live one long life being really nothing
> but absolutely nothing but mistaken and that makes them
> irritating if you feel that way about mistakes but certainly
> something that you can be continuously using and ev-
> erlastingly enjoying.

Can get itself in.
Can get itself out of the room.
Room without help room exigent.
Room structuralist room neoformalist there is no help room
language poet oriented the young bird is doomed 53, 33, 22,
19, 15, 7 and so on from five up to 52 yet we are loving you
period no we cant say that period.

> Poetry is concerned with using with abusing, with losing
> with wanting, with denying with avoiding with adoring
> with replacing the noun. It is always doing that, doing
> that and doing nothing but that. Poetry is doing nothing
> but using losing refusing and pleasing and betraying and
> caressing nouns. That is what poetry does, that is what
> poetry has to do no matter what kind of poetry it is. And
> there are a great many kinds of poetry.

Without a sense of words intact abstract from memory's stuff
we will obey the rules that is here darling period.
Diamond-shaped the crystal grazing Hereford theorists period.
The bird we saw had the sense to fly out.
We make a note without question it perched.
It perched on the window it flew right into I ask you.

I ask you can we use you for our all investigations now period.
And shall we.
And shall we sing a song against the rules
What is your answer Gertrude Stein? question mark period tell.

> I recognize verbs and adverbs aided by prepositions and
> conjunctions with pronouns as possessing that whole of
> the active life of writing.

PRIMITIVE ROAD

My dream was all at night. And as dreams are at night, you can barely see color. Where did it start? Where it started not with the getaway. But the dream was all getaway. You see it had been a surprise who did it, we didn't expect the hero of the bible to appear as if he were the hero of the resistance, to catch a thief. The hero of the bible appeared and then we knew it was all a pose. Two policemen had been shot at close range, at so close range, it was right in front of us, we saw it. We'd already been arrested and let go before. Then Jesus Rosenberg walks down the ramp in black leather claiming the blame. Did we dress in expensive clothing to cross the border into Mexico, did we have a good enough car to get away with it, three men and one woman, did Ted give me a hat that looked like a fried egg but was actually a tape recorder, did we pack food for the trip and dress carefully as if it were another dream where we wore the clothing of the rich, borrowed them and then had to give them back, all soiled and muddy, we also drank in my dream.

It was hard to know what to take with us for life and we packed cold ham and potatoes efficiently and with a kind of energy I enjoy dreaming about though the murders had seemed as superfluous and even gratuitous as did the appearance of David or Jesus on the boardwalk jauntily claiming the blame. We weren't edgy, we just figured we had to stay out of jail. And so this dream stays with you beyond the waking hours and only persists with clothing to change into and out of, repeatedly, until the sense of the dream wears off, you can change clothing, all day if you want, you can spend alot of time deciding what to wear as if it were as important as this, being the last time we will have a choice, a chance to change our clothing at all, in jail we wear only the same issued things, here is a little variety and even maybe color in the dream, an orange and blue shirt, white pants, seen in the bright indoor light, the dark green night. But what difference does it make, I enjoy writing it all down, and even would wish for more detail, perhaps a detailed recounting made at dawn and then again later with all the changes of the dream's half sleep, but it's not something I feel deeply about. Even the appearance of David, a shallow character at best in the dream, indicating to me that this was the dream's purpose, to present this man with the name of another man, in all the clothing and all the trappings of not only a biblical man and a criminal but a complete surprise, as if to remind me I've not been paying my dues, as they say, and just as you might forget all about your pointless religion, especially on a Sunday, so I've been looking like I've forgotten all about this man, yet my mind is saying nevertheless, he stills lays claim to all the blame. All the blame there. But what does it mean to me to think this or be reminded of it. And here it is all in the further clothing of a Hitchcock thriller I couldn't stay

awake for. I don't enjoy writing about why I can't write some-
thing or about something but I must say that poetry escapes me
when strong feelings just do not seem to be around, and so this
must be a weakness in a way. All this spring, though I find
myself observing the spring most exactly and more so than
ever in my memory, the formations of the little buds from their
very beginnings to the openings of whole new trees on each
branch and the cupped clusters that so surprisingly seem to
make leaves and then when they make them, they make them
in such abundance and so sturdily and fast that one sees as last
why a tree can so strongly resemble nothing else and how
casual the leaves are in their numbers, ten or twenty coming
out of each new cluster that was last a fist and how different
areas of the town and country have all these things happening
in different stages and at different times depending on whether
it's a cold spot or a warm one and how each bud on a tree
branch can truly be called a blossom at a certain point and all
the kinds can be observed as closely and in as distinct stages as
the ferns unfolding from fiddleheads, getting to that point
where they look like graceful hands with an offering or even
holding a pen, and some trees are late bloomers, so there is a
reason for that phrase, and the trees in this stage being then
more interesting to observe than the flowers that come up and
bulge out so fast, practically overnight, and the trees that get
caught in storms and lose branches over me, lose whole
branches with nests of bad caterpillars on them, yet there are
the whole fields of flowers, bluets I'm told, that one can lie
down in as on velvet, but the ground is more strewn with
branches from the last storm and when you crack them they're
wet and almost white inside though the leaves have become
brittle and memory now retells which are the truly dead trees in

the neighborhood, still hanging out for the sake of their beauty
I suppose on the horizon, so though I see all this and wonder at
the men and women who can mow the dandelions down and all
the bluets with them, for the sake of an idea of unadulterated
green and grass that is short and not conducive to bugs and
mosquitoes, and we had a bee in today, I still can't feel as
strongly about it as I do when something tells me I'm about to
see the year's first big snow. As if for the sake of alertness
maybe, I can steel myself then and let fall in a minute every-
thing I've stored or gotten like a hermit or a squirrel from the
sun and the green, not that I ever understand what I'll do after
that, when the gray qualities of November really begin to take
over nor even to speak of the tediousness of early February, so
much more inspiring to me than any part of June. Perhaps it's
that the possibility of normal activity and the freedom from
heavy clothing somehow lessen my ability to feel concise or
that I have something to offer to my room and work that is
completely unique, here indoors where it is really all my own.
So if we must really share the sights of ourselves, twentieth-
century-style, we are all becoming a little bit too accepted or
ordinary, I am a mother and you are a father, brick is com-
monly used to build houses and fireplaces. My brick heart
hasn't done anything yet this spring, it quickened in readiness
for spring, around early March, March 1st to be exact I felt it
quickening but I've still got ice around the door. I saw a house
today, now this is the middle of May yet we did have a snow-
storm last week, but it's been truly warm since, and in one of
this house's corners was a modest pile of snow, dirty snow
even. It was an ugly fascist-type house, architecturally severe
and almost windowless, and kept in such good order by its
owners on the outside that it had no charm at all, as if the idea

of life were to create new areas out of the beautiful wild that had to be constantly tended yet needed no use. Now if a wildness of a profusion is used or not used, in the best sense it still will look the same, that is the beauty of it. Marie can pull up bluets all day from the woods or even from the wild gardens and they will never be the worse for having met a baby that nobody had to say no to. This reminds me of something somebody once said to me about women's bodies being used or not used, that is for having children, but that is a much trickier subject though it's true I know a few women who are wild-looking beyond use and not depending on it in that sense, and I admire their looks very much. And men too, I suppose people in general can indeed look planned or even weeded and not meant for use, I could even say for lying down in, and then that is a very annoying way of looking. I saw alot of old women today at a garden party and though their faces were all very interesting to observe, they seemed to be to a man dressed in inhumanly colored pant suits and stiff shoes that would cause a child to scream in pain. "Are your feet complaining too?" I heard one woman say to the other. So the fascist house deserved its patch of snow and I hope it was still there from the whole winter and not just this final recent storm. I think when I don't observe the smaller goings on of the season or when the season is pressing towards being a scene for only major happenings, I feel more greatly toward it. And when I see all this profusion and life in other ways going on very well without any push from me, well, the trilliums are even growing there beyond my sight in Aspinwall Park and I've yet to see ice that can't be cracked invisibly as I move my face closer to the window and breathe. Even for love we need to go to work and sit mediations and show ourselves, take all our clothing off, and the more the better. This spring has come too easily, in the face of too hard a winter, to be too pretty, too overwhelming when you get up close, it even dares to be windy and cold. Even for love I think you have to stay warm all the time when you're supposed to be warm, otherwise the other person, that's me, will start doing something else, like cleaning up the room.

A NON-UNIFIED FIELD THEORY OF LOVE AND LANDLORDS

Billions of tiny catastrophes
occur as the photons
randomly entering your eyes
each second you read this
land on your retina

Tiny space dusts and space grains of sand rain
Down on the earth by the millions each minute
And interplanetary and interstellar comets ast
Eroids and meteoroids are more numerous than a
Ll the fish in all the seas of the world and y
Ou might discover a comet and become famous an
D in recent years we've begun to learn that th
E universe might be less peaceful than we want
To think and things often happen by chance and
Are manifested as great disasters and authorit
Y used for any other purpose than service lead
S to corruption, this is a lush fantasy and in
Some cases 113 is the same as 74 and chaos and
catastrophe become the rule and not the except
Tion and Hyperion is not alone, according to D
R. Wisdom's latest work and when a moon breaks
Out of a locked mode, trumbling can ensue, phys

Icists see progress in moving beyond simple ch
Aos to "macho turbulence" and I'm not sure if
You would want me to take more liberties in ma
King changes, so as to avoid so many questions
In the future. Please let me know. Someday s
Omething will collide with the earth and cause
The whole world to shake and the skies to dark
En and the oceans to overrun the continental L
owlands and intense shock waves have bizarre p
Alm-tree-like formations and meteorites have a
Tendency to fall most heavily in the afternoon
And it would take $11\frac{1}{2}$ days to count to a milli
On and to count to a billion it would take 32
Years without sleeping and for colds put a sma
Ll carrot in each nostril or tie raw onions to
Your feet, you know, wandering pieces of space
Ice rock and metal prove we are finite and coi
Ncidences are the rule in this universe and sc
Ientific method is fallible but it's our only
Reasoning scheme he said and logic is perfect
By default and mathematics is almost perfect
And physical science is far from perfect and s
Omeone said I dont want to know everything for
Fear I will end up like the old man and the yo
Ung boy who lost their minds on the mountain p
Eaks and for snoring, tickle the snorer's thro
At and sleep with your feet to the south, I'm
Telling you things in this universe are flying
Around in unimaginably complex ways, you don't
Even believe I love you and eventually one pie
Ce of wood will refuse to burn and strangely,

tiny space dusts and space grains of sand rain
down on the earth by the millions each minute,

Tumbling results from precisely the same gravi
Tational laws and tidal forces that cause moon
S to lock into a stable orbital resonance with
Their planets and things wrap around and get m
Ixed up and entangled with one another and his
Tory is full of examples of professors ousted
From their positions and Giordano Bruno was bu
Rned at the stake, Galileo put under house arr
Est and the discoverer of transfinite cardinal
S was driven insane by the establishment's mis
Treatment and if you cant sleep spray your hop
S pillow under which you've put a raw onion wi
Th alcohol while drinking goats' milk filled w
Ith boiled crabs and in an average lifetime ha
Ir grows twenty-five feet and chaotic behavior
Is the flip side of the Newtonian coin and Zeu
S rhymes with zoos and I have a teapot with a
Dragon on it and if you turn it around there's
bird-fish in an ocean-sky and eggs can be stoo
D upright quite easily in late March and Sept.
But it is nearly impossible to accomplish this
In December or June and mathematics teaches lo
Ve's theorems of least upper bound and greates
T lower bound, that is, if a statement is fals
E and then becomes true, it must change state
At a single instant and how is the universe pu
T together and how is love put together and ho
W are landlords put together and how did the u

Niverse come to be and how did love come to be
And how did landlords come to be and someday t
He human race will have to move to another sol
Ar system in the Milky Way or in some other ga
Laxy because of the deterioration of the sun a
Nd then we will have to move again because the
New sun will begin to die and then we will hav
E to move again like a transient apartment dwe
Ller who always has some problem with his land
Lord

THE LANDLORD QUIT TO WRITE A BOOK

What happened that night?
Cake calming the library
More proportioned than a pregnancy
As of the crusty pyramid you sent me
To ward off fictional love, that is,
The brighter the light you stare at
The more pernicious the symbolizing eggs
What held the tags on the whale?

What color was her dress?
They havent stopped coming looking for water
Are they celebrities? The people of darkness?
A flat form, miles wide and intellectual
Has died one of those deaths in hospitals
What awakened me?

What glowed in the night?
Hating himself more for his girth than his greed

The landlord quit his job to write a book
On the subject of the vanishing rainforests
How many children left their homes?

In how many ways are seeds scattered?
Single, Sagittarius male, 60s, self-employed, divorced,
    occasional smoker, drinker, likes the outdoors. Seeks
    female companion from the Philippine Islands, the Orient
    or Hawaii, who would like to relocate
How many rooms were in the house?

What kind of leaves has sugar cane?
Born-again Christian woman, 31, single, never married,
    enjoys family life, serving God, hard work, home,
    Bible study, writing, sewing, animals, teaching,
    making Christian videos. Seeks marriage-minded man.
    No smoker, drinker, drug-user, nor divorced man
    need reply
What writhed?

What was the total number of eyes the monster had?
A genuine actual diamond encased in real gold gold
Plus a one-time-only pill for eternal health, beauty
& immortality are yours for just five dollars plus postage
If you order within seventy-two biblical hours,
Are a citizen, and your name begins with P, Q, S or T
Whose home was in the pool?

The coldest day recorded at the South Pole was how many
    degrees below zero?
Theodore was never conscious of the meaning of his name

Theodore & Dorothy were never conscious of etymologies
All their lives he called her Dolly; she him Teddy
For thirty dollars I will give you my umbrella
For sixty dollars worldwide peace, omnipresent freedom
What froze?

What got very hot?
Astonishing natural bridges five hundred feet long
Remove the effect of illegitimacy from a sweet fruit
Though he gave himself to other men, especially song writers,
I exchange for a good dinner, in this he was not unlike many
& now no one but the famous hustler will be named as his lover
How many men survived?

Who gave the party?
Finally dinner was over & the dishes and glasses
Were washed & put away & the cabinet doors closed
The house looked again as if it had never been used
The people in it went to bed and then to sleep
Root crops should be planted in which period of the moon?

PROPER NAME

A man in a shirt showing a man in a shirt a shirt is how many white shirts are there there. Here's 11²/₃ yds. writing which is wiring meant to be performed not read off the page as pole high-wire act performs as the feeling of not being subject had put who into a different act which was a different danger was a different risk, the riskier text than the lecture the riskier word not heard & pinched, no way out but the way in, leaving: "who's dead?" I wont use names, names are not use, I wont name names, all names begin with F. Crazy F. & frenzied F. & fucking F. & dead F. & dead fucking F. & the anagrams of all the letters that follow F. in the names named, relate here, that is, they send the image of a man off to sea with the sails sails flow around & where they do, fucking F. So, if all names begin with F. then F. = Proper Name: nobody can stand it. We pass by glass windows of Proper Name's family's summer house by the water & they're drinking again so this has no title, except, the blue edge of the surf defines something & I attempt to make

its words communicable its surf communicable, I season its
fucking concept by painting it green & therefore making no
change. Proper Name or Proper Name is leaning weary against
the bed & sitting on the floor there, doll & doll then, she gets
very drunk, yes she does & she gets very drunk then she has a
man in. You could sink in sex is not a person's name at all.
And we're there but everybody leaves. A man in a shirt show-
ing a man in a shirt is how many white shirts are there there.
You put your work first & try to do everything all at once so
that you can be sure that everything has no meaning but all at
once does, as, the red rose doesnt the rose is red does, and, it's
a strange city, morning & just as I'm poaching scrambled eggs
& boiling bottled coffee cups for coffee for them they leave,
as, once when they were nearly ready, they had ordered it to
close, as she gets very drunk then she has a man in. So sex wait
for me, they're walking down the street & I have to pack &
should I leave all my fucking things here & I would I say I
would except I dont mean it cause there's a book in each bag &
a bag in each book & I need the book in each bag & all the
fucking junk, along with all the fucking junk, there is, where
there is. & so what so crawling through white excavation evac-
uations, 40,000 trampled to death over one couple of lovers
yelling for help wake up. A set. A magazine full of nothing but
a book by me called something starring Proper Name & on the
back it says, book jacket, this writing was discovered written
by moon-discovered hands by Proper Name through Proper
Name, or something like that, as, one tame tiger does not exist.
But, no one knows this. The walking cure. I just thought of it I
havent told anyone. I feel very C & Proper Name feels very H
in the middle of all this two people, a man & a woman in a
cemetery erasing a tombstone & this has nothing to do with this

Proper Name Proper Name Proper Name Proper Name &
Proper Name, beside the two others, or, in the same space but
with a space between, etc. There's a fire escape hydrant which
offers all different kinds of water fountains drinking fountains
drinking fountains, I drink from one, choke & am forbidden. I
wake up to the sexual etiology of the child where, not quite yet,
shit this is some mystery novel, where the women place on the
team. I leave off playing basketball & Proper Name comes &
takes my place & I come back I want my place back but she's
the open man & she's the open man around so I fuck Proper
Name & Proper Name who is also Proper Name at once & this
is the harsh creation of the deprivation of moralism of the
moralism of deprivation of the relaxation of a deprivation of
the excitement of relaxation of the excitement of a deprivation
it's a kiss & Shakespeare's shrine is a composite image. We
visit it, it's my shrine. Women take care of it, it's falling apart.
They rush to get a room ready for visitors & there's no hope of
that cause in the existence of the predicate it was the predicate I
forgot so Proper Name called to remind me that tame tigers
growl & it's tame tigers growl. Other shrines appear & their
shapes all lead in the same direction shown showing a birthday
party shown outdoors as a picnic on the streets for one alone
woman who is alone & she's alone. Everybody's there, we
come & Proper Name & his wife come & we're introduced & I
lean back & do my perfect Proper Name imitation: ''Hello
Proper Name, cut short.'' The derivative of a Proper Name &
its parent the derivative of a Proper Name. These people are all
dead. You get dead. Where are my shirts made of different
materials with the arms different from the torsos & the backs
different from the fronts. Where are my man-woman shirts & I
have alot of them & who's got that one & nevermind, I have

another one it's green it's painted green like the dress in the sex show. Somebody broke the lighter & all the details get care as the women place on the team as this is dreaming of everything I can think of, as, I dream you drink up all the fucking milk & in fact you do. In the beginning you know why I cant begin to write cause it would be the bad writing of secrets the evil throwing up of them the giving them up the catching & replacements are catching they catch you up in what recurs to you, its disgusting its filth its beginning so, they carry me there, door to door: Proper Name to Proper Name with Proper Name in between whose door I also go out by. Proper Name, Proper Name & Proper Name I wish I could, fuck you, through the park, to lay that on there, to lay that on you, lay that one on you & dont wanna use the loaded words wanna come up with the loaded ideas so wait & just say it again, as, the shirts the table just bite it off, some euphoria, concentrating on you & my objects, as, is it as difficult for men not to have children at all as it is for me, dear Proper Name Proper Name Proper Name Proper Name Proper Name & Proper Name & those are the ones I wanted to create one night, who's first. And it's hard to concentrate, I burned myself, Proper Name works in a frenzy of work & then lets himself down which reminds me of Proper Name & so now I'm worried about him & about the fact that this is not writing, when you know so much already, as, once when they were nearly ready, they had ordered it to close. Like emotions, A to Z, I feel very S. But I want to explain the difference, in fucking, between a creation & a deprivation, two states & how they are the same & these are my notes, why should I know them, the child knows them. A creation, your word, it cant be someone you know. & the idea that writing should be working at something & reworking & revising &

someone says that fucking is it should be difficult it's work I dont agree, fucking off completely. It's easy to fuck. Nobody gets hurt by fucking but madmen & madwomen. Is that true. My hunger creates a food that everybody needs. You or me? And the excitement is different. In a way, in this way, it's the excitement that needs to be created & it doesnt need to be satisfied, is not sex, is. Tame tigers growl. They do not exist. Is not language, is. And the same harshness in both, stone white stone cold stone stoned a warm stone. I will have you to generate my excitement as the only way I can & so, I'll do anything for you & in the process to complete the scene of the crime, let me fill all your desires full & then, so you'll love me oddly, by force, afterwards, forever as the work ethic. This is some communication, you dont need to know my history. A teacher in the worst sense but she leaves their minds alone. And so, Proper Name's frenzy is between the excitement of a deprivation & the heightening the drama & the melody & that same excitement made by a dreadful falling of affection on & this is like Proper Name. And so, Proper Name of the dream, I think, the double Proper Name at once. Either way it's drama, in the deprived state & in the dreadful falling of affection state & this is peculiar because I thought in this second state, the dreadful falling of affection state, I would still be taking about fucking & I am not. Fucking, with Proper Name who is not Proper Name either & with my Proper Name character who is not quite or not exactly Proper Name, only takes place in the dreadful falling state & what has this got to do with me, falling. Fucking, I am alone here in the house now I am not alone, somehow cures the deprived state or at least moves it over for a while & why deprived unless you feel you ought to be & this is where it gets back to me & sex & tame tigers growling & once when they were nearly ready, though I dont see how, I just know it from remembering my childhood. I'm lost so lost how lost can you be when everywhere you go it's morning & the sun's coming up over a map. Now, in both those statements of states there is something I've begun to describe as excitement & they seem to have this in common, an excitement that seems like sex but somehow isnt, in both the dreadful falling & the dreadfull falling. As if the need for needing sex needed to be aroused & that's all. In fact I have (never in my life), except for my childhood, fucked. Unless caught by surprise. And that is all there is of this myth of mine, see below. This is the sexual etiology of the child. She wants heroin. The I-character is usually the she. Let me just go quickly through pinpointing the fantasies, touch on each one. There was the blowjob, the heroin, touch tongues, the list of men, the dance-modeling scene, the violent scene in your office & the one in the country. The first three are real & were the touchstones of the others. More came later. I came home. Quick blowjob want heroin think of touch tongues. The list of men. I was trying to think of a man who would grab me. No, first I'm tough I think of Proper Name & wonder what grabs me to him suddenly, it's the way he grabs you, pins you down, at least he pinned me down, without even knowing me, just right, not for then & not for then but for now, why. I go through the list & try to think who could do it, it's nothing that I could do at all, nothing for me to do, it has to be done, I think maybe Proper Name could do it but no. He couldnt do it, I imagine presenting myself as the vulnerable object at Proper Name's new loft. When is he moving in, saturday. I'll go up there, I'll just arrive, but he always has so many women around, no he doesnt it's just an illusion he makes, he's a prick too, there wont be anyone there,

I'll go up there & wait for him to do it, in fact I'll explain to
him what I want. This is why Proper Name is perfect, he
wouldnt care, I'll explain to him what exactly what I want I
he'll do it, no it'd be better if Proper Name could do it, no it'd
be better if I just waited for Proper Name to grab me & start to
fuck, the whole thing, no, I dont want to fuck I just want him to
grab me, that'd be enough, just the grabbing by the arm &
maybe the pinning down, I'd escape. Proper Name couldnt do
it, he'd laugh, Proper Name'd be too serious, I couldnt be
serious with Proper Name & Proper Name would just freak
out, more trouble, too much to bear for him, he'd say she's
crazy, I thought so & just like all the other ones I've been
involved with & so on. I'll go to the poetry reading & see
who's there, there'll be somebody there who'll be perfect, not
Proper Name, he's too nice & doped. I know the perfect one;
it's Proper Name, but I dont like him. Proper Name. Or the
poetry reading. Just cruising. As usual. This is where she sort
of branches off for good in the bed. Hours must've been going
by. She's modeling a new sort of dress in a new kind of sex-
show-modeling-show, it's the dress you center your attention
on, watch: she comes out onto the stage in the dress. Do you
want to know what the dress is like? I'll describe it later.
There's a man, close on her heels, she's got no shoes on, no, I
put that in later. She walks to center-stage, the man behind her.
He twists her arm & pushes her out onto the runway: it's a
thrust stage: this is where you got to see the front of the dress.
She acts in pain. The man, keeping hold of the twisted arm
behind her back, grabs her breast with his other hand, it's a
low-cut dress, maybe he even lets one side of the dress drop
down, he keeps his hand on her breasts, her act of pain changes
a little towards pleasure, an ache, but the moment this hap-

pens, this change in her attitude, this lessening of the pain you can see in her face, he turns her around: This is where you get to see the back of the dress. It's black, low-cut like I said & full-length, maybe her leg can be seen through a slit up the side of the dress, maybe he caresses her thigh during the act, but the black of the dress as it falls turns to violent red & then purple, the brightest deepest shades, & the back, in shades of the same quality, the back is deep blue & green, the dress is like a tree, it must be painted, she is very credible because she is in her act, will people laugh at her, they dont. He turns her around & takes her hair which falls down her back & pulls it forward so you can see the cut of the dress, she does nothing but act, her movements are directed. The man & woman speak but cant be heard, you have seen the back of the dress, then the walk back down the runway to center-stage & here, if I forget exactly how I staged it, it doesnt matter, here is where I put in she is barefoot, cause she runs away, she runs to stage left & here you see the beautiful dress moving, & when she reaches a certain point she stops, gives a look of total desperation to the man across the stage & just as this look is passing across her face, she begins to extend her arms outward to take a slight bow, her head bends down after a brief look at the audience, a look without pain. And just as she has begun this bow, the man, reaching across the stage, extends his arm in her direction indicating that she take her bow: this is done so that there is no doubt that the performance is over & that the dress is for sale. Now that is all there is of that. The consequences of this scene bring us back to something real, like the list of men, combined with something less real & this is what it is. But first I have to introduce a new character, the Proper-Name-God, el, al aaraaf, israfel, ishmael, Proper Name thy beauty is, but I am like a stone & the Proper-Name-character begins to be the he-character even though some of the feminine engenders a kind of relief from that being true directly, you see, he must be a sister-love to do this. She will use his office to set the scene. It's raining out & she becomes hysterical, she is out of control. & he hits her, there's less embellishment, there's none, he simply hits her, you dont have to know why, it's the only thing he can do, he hits her, I put in a reason why, it comes later. He hits her & she hits him back. & this infuriates him & this is where I put in the reason why, it's cause he is out of control too, he loses control even more than she does, out of frustration, this is the reason I put in here, & I put it in because he gets so infuriated that he punches her, his fist is big enough to hit her mouth, cheek & the lower part of her eye all at once, he hits her really hard & she falls down. He moves across the room, not looking, she starts to bleed, maybe she loses a tooth, she's dazed, falls down, starts to get up, spits out a tooth, she wipes her face with her shirt & remembers there's a door to a kind of garden or backyard behind his chair, she makes for it, he tries to stop her, the table gets knocked over, the lamp, he grabs her, she puts her head down. There are all kinds of things that could happen next, what I'm saying is there were many variations, like, the noise brings somebody down from upstairs, there's a scene like talking between doors, or he goes out to take care of it but cant because she'll run out into the yard, or there's someone waiting to see him & he tells them there's an emergency, you see, he cant let her get away. It's obvious he cant cause there's this incredible bruise beginning to show on her face & blood & a black eye, she's very happy about it, what can he do with her. Maybe he even takes her upstairs, maybe no one's home, maybe no one's waiting to see him & it goes on

forever, go over it again, maybe he even has to call up some-
one on the phone, bring in a new character, there is another
character involved with this, no, it's just between these two,
what can they do next. Nothing, there's nothing to follow it, el,
al aaraaf, israfel, ishmael, the only one left, wants to suffer. In
the country. In a room. I wont put this part of how I proceeded
on paper. Do you assume in your creation that humans have an
understood love to begin with & when I get that from you, I
can make you any one, another, even the persecutor, I ask this
because from here I went on, it's so clear in my mind, to the
thing, the idea, so clear in our minds, & how do I put it down
here, no way. Something about being in the country together in
a room. We're there & we make love, for the first time in
months in my mind, do you have me, & there's no need to
detail this fantasy cause the details I created were so inter-
changeable I had to go over it again & again, I wanted to bring
in all the possibilities, you undress first, I undress first, you
undress, I do, I undress you, you undress me, I'm afraid to go
much further except that I had stayed up all night dreaming
violence so that we could get to this room, & this, I touched
your penis, we did everything. I couldnt decide whether we did
it all in one night, or whether we had time, whether we went to
the forest, whether it was next spring: I'm really glad you got
to be Proper Name, you cant get away that easy, I'll stay up all
night for years to clear up this mess & make Proper Name.
That is the sexual etiology of the child. Another table. Because
of another table. Another picnic table. Proper Name-Proper
Name-Proper Name, a composite of helplessness, is sitting
there next to me & someone, I, start(s) to cry & it goes like a
rattle down the length of the table, all the way to, & at this
point Proper Name, the strong part, extends her leg & shows us

her mechanical leg-part built into her thigh: all the transistor-like electronic pieces are exposed like an open tape recorder & its insides & this somehow permits her/me to move & speak words, & it goes like a rattle down the length of the table, all the way to a man, even a man, crying, no, he jolts up, says what, nothing. It was an involuntary jerk, on his part & not a cry (crying). And this is called Proper Name's Death. And there's more. It's Proper Name walking around, her sick self, when she would walk around watching intently walking but too weak to move somehow also intently watching & I feel like I am always going back to her, visible, in the dream & in the dream I say, yes, she was in the other dream yesterday too & then, all the dreams, watching intently walking, in the dream room. I met her somewhere on the face of the map & now she's checking on my traveling. And this is called why I cant move. And by an intense effort of the memory I remembered to hit Proper Name in the face for all that watching & I am in a loft which is a commune & where there is going to be a performance. I cant do anything private here & first we get coffee, a new kind that you have to squeeze the coffee in a piece of cheesecloth or filter with your hands into your cup. It's no good. There are cheeseburgers but something keeps happening to the food. We dont get it. Alot of people are beginning to filter in for the show & I think this is where I hit Proper Name. I see Proper Name, a helpless old friend of Proper Name's who spent alot of time in a mental hospital once, another one, & this is the one & this is the dream I understand least about, another one, & it's Proper Name's commune. I investigate it as a possible place to live. I see a girl in a trailer, possibly living alone. You can squeeze the coffee but not Proper Name. And this is the dream I understand least about. Proper Name &

Proper Name, both of them dead, property is theft. And so, we cross the low stone wall in the snow between East & West Germany at great danger to ourselves & some ghost tries to grab my foot as I'm almost over & we go eat in an outdoor restaurant. We order wine & are smoking. They tell us the rules: you can drink wine if you dont smoke & smoke without wine but not both, but if one of you isnt drinking then you can all smoke, because that person can smoke. & this is East Germany. No tame tigers exist. It seems to have more to do with the ashtrays than any idea. The landscape is a town of condemned armories, X's on the windows, an emotion, some smashed. To get in you have to prove you've had a baby so there's a store on the border sells baby clothes & people who bought them to prove it throw them away on their way back out. And this is called property is robbery. And so, Proper Name & I are in a room, dreaming. Proper Name & I are in a room, cleaning. Cleaning benches & tables furiously. Furiously green ideas go to sleep. Tame tigers growl. She suggests harshly that we live together on harsh terms. And later I erect, but first I am reading at a reading of Odd Poetry with all the other ones, they are Proper Name's friends. I'm not nervous, I read automatically without feeling. I read second or third & then leave. I have no idea of it being good or bad. And this is called the end of the idiot. & Proper Name pans Heat. Later I erect a stone castle-room within the room we were cleaning & in one half of it I cover the windows with the green castle-curtains that divide the room of the end of the idiot. You are always truthful, so, you are never fair. And this is called the end of the idiot. Proper Name is the star of a movie. His performance is a success & he's funny. And this is called Proper Name is now the star of the movie.

IS SUMMER THERE?

One more time like the cold wind it's icy
There's a dream that won't leave me alone
I'm putting on my coat because there's nothing to it
The alcohol evaporates into thin air
No one notices I have only one eye
I am cheated of pleasure and denied by constancy
I'm ashamed of weakness, betrayed by strength
I belong nowhere, I am without a thought
The more I do the more my imperfect heart
Demands recuperation from its obsession
Do you think Clair has left her husband?
Shall I bring the red tray with me tomorrow
To use as a slide? Tell me what is it?
Will I survive, am I a derelict already?
Everyone knows me I seem to know no one
Nothing happens, nothing is an adventure
But nothing is calm, I am forbidden to be here,

Lost on a path alone out in the cold
Even its drama is misleading, I'm misdirected
So I pretend to see nothing, I have a memory
Of what I probably see, I go on that,
Nothing is ordinary, the problem is perfection
I'll write a song to do away with all of it
I only sing whatever I fear is nothing
I fear I'm forbidden to sing and I dream I sing
I dream again I can't find what there is to eat
I dream I sing it's love that is misleading me
And all love's lent to the song in a kind of weakening,
I wait to find out and I find out nothing,
Old age or disappearance or desertion
I would do anything to be among you,
To love you more lightly to receive
Ordinary love spent more thoughtlessly,
This writing is not love it is beneath love,
I put it down on paper because it's surer
Than love I've seen isolating me like fear
When I'm only doing ordinary walking
And I should be going from place to place.

ELEGY

When we were thirteen we began
To go to shcool by subway,
We took the 7:10 a.m. elevated train
From the Forest Avenue station in Ridgewood, Brooklyn,
Where there was a pot-bellied stove in the waiting room
Where lights flashed to signal an oncoming train on the platform,
To Broadway and Myrtle where you didn't have to change
      trains
If you had gotten on a steel train, they ran in rush hours.
At the Broadway station the train got packed
With phony nuns with big breasts and pom-poms instead of
      rosaries
And men who made the whole train odorous with garlic,
Then they would rub their erections up against us girls
Till we got to the hell-hole of Essex and Delancey Streets
Where we would run through tunnels with hordes of other
      people

To get the downstairs train, the D-train to Park Slope.
When we got off at 9th Street there was always an exhibitionist
Waiting in the stairway to show the girls his penis,
Once in a while the semi-cloistered nuns would get wind of this
And he would disappear for a while, he was never erect.
On the way home on the train in the late afternoon
Occasionally a gang like the Halsey Bops or even the Baldies
Would rampage through the train and break all the lightbulbs,
Then when it was time to get off at your stop
They'd pretend they wouldn't let you till the last minute
Or if you were on the train on a date at night
The gangs would mostly harass the guys and call them queers.
When I worked at St. Vincent's I'd get on the train at dawn
And connect with the Canarsie Line at Wyckoff Avenue,
Then we'd always get stuck under the river with crazy lunatics
Who just had to pee into somebody's shopping bag,
Then later the police with such visible guns you thought to take
        them
Began to be around the subways with all their gear and walkie-
        talkies.
The Delancey-Essex Streets station was always full of men
Without legs on skateboards who were begging, they had
        signs,
And when we went to the end of the Myrtle Avenue line
To go to A&S's the whole walk to the store from the train
Was lined with beggars sitting up against buildings with their
        crutches
And nuns shaking tambourines and singing, also begging,
Someone once told me some of these people weren't real.
The other end of the el at Metropolitan Avenue in Queens
Was a scene like the country with grass growing on the tracks.

I was always most scared of the West 4th St. & Houston St.
        stations
And the ones on the Canarsie line on either side of the river,
I think it's Bedford St. & Graham Avenue, it's a long time in
        between,
Once I fell asleep and went under the river in error,
I had to get out to get back in to turn around
But the gates of the station on the other side were locked
So I was forced to go even further in the wrong direction
Or else I'd die, I've never gotten hurt on the subways
Though I've been scared by people with guns and knives
And I've slipped and fallen on the subway stairs
And later I became afraid of the subways in a neurotic way
Because it was the kind of place I thought I couldn't get out of
And the light and noise & atmosphere made me feel crazy.
I'm always mesmerized when I see a baby on the subways
Or the big families you see there alot on Sundays,
I've always thought I might get caught in one of those things
Where you put your token when there's no token booth,
Once when I was mesmerized by love I took the subway home
        alone
In the middle of the night and when I got to 14th Street
And the recording started saying, ''Please stand clear of the
        moving
Platform,'' and so on, there was an announcement there were
        no more trains
That night going south except non-stop to the Battery and
        beyond
So I got out and walked the rest of the way home to Grand
        Street
In what I felt was an imitation of the rhythm of the train

But I forget how I did it and if you asked me today
To get on a subway I'd pretend I was going to if I had to
And then out of fear I'd either walk or if I had the money
I'd go buy a beer and hail a cab, I don't know why.
Memories have always seemed as senseless and dramatic
As any crime, there's no crediting the present for that.
Naive as a girl I saw alot in the subways, now all that is over,
The wooden trains weren't as heavy as the ones made of steel
And there was always the question of the fragility of the el.
The stairs were steep and it was a rush to make the train on time,
The token booths are concentration camps and you are alone,
It's easily the blue of the sky and the love of exercise
To vault the fence, to be warned, to meditate like expense
The smell of burning iron, the cleanliness of that flight
Through the useful subways to measure the time, to practically
  live there,
See what everyone is reading and pretend to be innocent when
  alone
Like as if to buy survival at the store and go on luck
In a place where you've seen everything at which you cannot
  look
Because then you would die or make a connection with the guy
Across the way in the tunnel without no sky like this writing
Or the violence of the day had to be all this pushing and
  fighting
And all the men and women were reading novels about fucking
Or romantic love in the escapist sense or the papers in Yiddish
  or Spanish
To transport love's wish to endure till we get there, surviving
As we do even flying on a big classy plane which is called
  arriving.

ATTENTION TO SPRING

Most human beings feel a pleasure after dinner
Of after whatever they have to eat is eaten
If there's enough of it and if food isn't love
Or something that it isn't
                              If I say more
I could say there's a thaw
And it's raining on the beaten snow like spring
Precociously missing the moment to get in

                              Neurotic spring,
Don't bother, we know we have to live through every day,
It's only early March, we don't need your protestations
Of an insistent love that means we'll pay later
Like the blizzard of 1888
                              We all know the weather
Is like friendship and love, I got a letter
Today like today's false spring
                              We are all going around

Saying we love the rain just because the air is warm
For once I have a friend in Fame

                            No I'm just kidding
But if I met Fame would Fame be a woman
Like the dinner or a man like the butcher

                                      I'd be wrong
If I said I'm not full of conceits
Conceits are far-fetched intricate amusements peculiar
To poetry, I say I thought I didn't know anything about it
Like the man or woman who next confesses the crime
In the image of love as parallel lines

                           Spring, I give up!
If you want to come intellectually today
I'll have you and on your terms I'll celebrate

                             But listen,
Love that won't endure won't be fair
I'm just sitting here, I had my dinner,
I'm not fainting, I'm your guest, I'm the subject
Of your manners & your genius

                       And though I'd like to say
I find this new way of stimulating conversation only titillating
And I beg love's truth from you like the sparrow I'll continue
To come over and talk anytime you ask me,

                           partly because
                               I'm hungry

And you set a good table
But mostly I admire your pretension to reason
And I find you inspiring and even eloquent

                           You once said
When I was faithless only constancy would impress you
Well here's my faith, it's no real dinner

But you have fed
Exacting memory now so equally as to lead me to dream
You might make a deal,

False host!
I am not your only intelligent guest!

0 TO 19

When you were born I was sucking at your young age your hateful love, the idiot of our starvation, my planned time to be. Sick that you took on my disease healthy as I was and pretended to cure it from your maleness right next to my helpless sorrow at your dying. I pretend I address idiots but I talk to normal people begging them with the charm I've got to simply be around, act busy and do things to convince me that not only, my dear nineteenth century and before, will the atomic bomb not fall on our heads as if it were our heads that thing might fall on (& is that an image of sadism too?) but also I forget what which proves I'm of this century and not from before, though doubt as of an animal or creature from outer space might enter in. My birth if such a word exists is the same as yours and this is addressed to you because to speak to somebody is so important, but to tell about oneself is dismal and often also the other word related to dismal which is failure. Now we are failures saluting our own selves for a split second in the shared belief, a phrase as hideous as the word hideous and as that nothing will ever change. I wonder if she believes that? Did she believe it before? Does she now? She who sits on the sinking dock excoriating her husband her lover who provides her with only money and comfort, she confides in me and I think of the time when I was born and then of the question of utterance—can it be true? If I speak to you now, not even knowing where you are since you're long dead and have a desire still to be living and I have a desire to write a book, this book, only for the dead, because my whole heart is not living and I dont know what life is like, I've never enjoyed life, have you? If I make this gentlemanly gesture as a woman to a man or men, will you add to it your own criticisms of what is really the truth at last? Or will you continue to withhold them and fight till the end for a dim-witted idea of your own personal honor, your lordliness, the stupid penis standing for strength or fortitude, standing up, when actually all the penis is is a great organ like in the Frick Museum (no children under 12 allowed). No I dont mean that, I dont mean to be mean, however I laugh at you misters and we all make speeches in our sleep in which we all lie down limply and with a graciousness and beauty not unlike avatarish death itself. Holy holy is the death of this trivial life without names. I will now mourn as I have done all my life since age eight of reasons like they say. I will mourn & I will mourn I will blow up trumpets and blow all the instruments and machines I will make no noise at all I will be dead as you are as a doornazi nail, this world was never nothing but to be & that is the same, mean and woman greed & practicality, occasional flumes of what is love known always as *the* flume. Why did you leave me? Impractical I sought to be born and was idiotically raised shy so that even beyond all the time it takes to get to be a grownup human and do something, I couldnt even say anything well past that time, I couldnt speak at all. We had been known to sing well or properly before that not speaking, we were admired for our tuneful singing, why we could imitate every song on the radio and in the right pitch, we did it for your amusement, that was love, to sing yet not to please, not to prolong life like a doctor. Remember the artful dodger? We stole from you, we took your most precious stuff, your breasts your beards your genitals we had them all for ourselves and in this world we owned them, they belonged to us, we stole them like fur stoles wrapped around your feeble bodies hoping to be richer someday, we might be! We wore you down, old eyes, false teeth already, the already stars had everything to do with it, you bought us a telescope to see to them beyond you. Did you not think when we looked through it that something amazing would happen, beyond the feeling of the backyards? Of the place or the people next door? It was presented as competitive like many things are, still are—you can see better than she, or she than he, or he than a she. Oh lioness outside my door you smiled wisely as the lion and didnt do anything but lead me around the house to the rooms I never knew existed there. American Indians came too to make all that clear and we stood in the center of our beds lying down remembering the ocean & knowing, I dont know why, that the floating on it was the same as the colors of the basement texts and garden doings. Had you not died young, you humans of colors, I dont doubt we would've been forced to die before you, as many did before their fathers in the age of cancer & car accidents & shit oh forget it other stuff. . . . I trail off here, you fools you immigrants sucked into the A&P, there was no money at all, there were fights about money, those were the only fights, there were no fights about love, there was no ostensible love, words are pure spinach. We ate the frozen lima beans when they were cold, watching the Philco T.V. out the corners of our punished eyes. The carrots are too earthy; some old people live on one can of soup a day. The children starve and the hole goes down to China. A my name is Arabelle and I live in Arcady I grow apples and my husband's name is Albany. We did climb mountains of a short sort once in a while and raced up them, one child succeeding better than the other in the competition for love. Even now the approval of a mass of diamond men stabs me like an engagement ring, the big sick nothing of an unarranged love. I wished for a brother, did you? We fought together and became quite gay. I can still imagine the brother I looked for, he looks like Matthew Tannenbaum actually, with much curly hair and kindly understanding of the world's problems and love of its pleasures. The paved front yard like the aerie of some eagles was surrounded like everything else with designs, this time of an overwrought iron gate and fences that did not open and close. Hard to try & make a life of it, to have so many cakes so much meat when you couldnt afford it, to have hobbies and retain dignity, to be a union man yet hate the union, to be a wife yet hate the wifeliness such loneliness yearning for the man who did something else, who didnt drive wildly in a carpool to Farmingdale who had no friends except at the Knights of Columbus, one of them was actually Italian, who went bowling, we lived in that house all our lives, that hateful house with the rows of laundry from each yard and window behind it, I know it used to be washed by hand, the water heated, then rolled through wringers and hung out to dry, no central heating. Coal had to be shoveled later, arcs of love it is enough to survive. We ran this way and that, always alone, getting lost in the graveyards and empty lot streets, having to walk miles back to where we began, nearest the delicatessen, the safe spot, the butcher, the church. Looked for beauty sort of in the vacant lots, found mostly in the library, but who cares? Strawberries were too hard to grow, then death encroached and ensued, oh fuck it. Who needs to hear all about it? One was born, whatever way, thought my mother was most beautiful-looking, admired her, laid on my father's cock on vacations, he said be careful, I slept with him, what difference does it make? Old hearty neuroticisms bent toward love, he must've enjoyed sleeping with me, I was Marie's age then, I find her lovely with her taut lean hard body, when I hold her up to leap into the water she's strong, no soft baby anymore to cuddle like Max is. If those guys thought I'd have a child named Max they'd've died. Funny thing is if Max'd been a girl he would've been named Theodora after one of you, unless we changed our minds. We went for two week vacations to places much like the place I'm in now with my family you guys've never seen, agglomerations of cabins in a no-class place by a lake. Housekeeping cabins they used to call them but they were different, now you rent them by the month, rather than by the week. Black Lake I saw you make love in, I wonder where it is. Probably you never made love there or anywhere, I doubt it so much. I'm not gonna defend you either, you were the most anxious people to have cars & t.v. sets despite your ideals which were probably none, you could have some things because you didnt have to pay rent. Meat you could have meat. & a pressure cooker plus we baked cakes & I'm not gonna tell about the port wine at holidays, so sickening and the big no-pleasure in everything but maybe to tell the truth nature, to see the trees once in a long while, to bear the brunt of them. To swim at Sunken Meadow State Park, till later someone said the black people went there. You are so long dead I cant imagine why I'm writing about you except for other deaths newer than yours, if there is such a thing. Idiotic vamps! The accompaniment of your tunes was just this dusk, and you too you added on lost ones. To tell of my born idiocy, so that I could be, well some people just tell what there is to tell without all this camouflage of green and eerie yellow designs in the wallpaper of the denizens of a certain part of brooklyn, now queens, where still below the suffrage of the moment lingers an anger so vehement as to make my association of myself with a beautiful looking candle of lavender or red orange seem an outrage to the humans who were my parents. Lucky others who've either got beyond this or never had to think about it, sweet staid place of death you linger in being now this moth now the other once a mother once a father, how come there werent more of you? A woman now I might love or a man. We knew you when. I have bottles in my hair; I dont expect my fingers which catch back to you. Writing is the most ridiculous thing to do. Now you do it of desire, now not. Who knows what it felt like in other times. To write and write, someone says write a sensible thing, some other a commercial. One is dead like the dead. We write and write thinking it's better than watching t.v. to attack the typewriter with love and anger faster to say all of memory and being, the future, maybe it doesnt exist. A word about kindness to be so. In all there is a joke now. & proceeding is idiocy like the saint or junkman. I went to school though nobody wanted me to. I too was much more fascinated with amusements than seeing the punishments that ensued from the nuns to the kids who peed out and over their wooden benches. We drew a lamp to honor them over a desk like ours with two people sitting at it playing cards or making a drawing, stick people in neat ways of being. Scariest figures of human faces ensconced in black and white stiff stuff fingering rosaries at their waists like ever-masturbating things in robes of masochistic pleasures, just pull them up, spank them and make them come, Sister Mary Magdalena, oh stations of the cross how severe it is to be tortured and nailed, please raise your hand if you are willing to suffer and die for your faith and what do you think of Joe McCarthy, hide under your desks when the bomb falls, we will teach you how, and what do you think of General MacArthur and the painting of the blue boy and all that we have not taught you? Please take the milk and distribute it since you're so smart, oh there's some modesses I save them in case any of the girls get their periods, I put them in my drawer, your sister is so much smarter than you are and you are so much smarter than she, since your blouse is ironed, even though you dont have a fresh blouse every day and you are smart you can sit in the first row and help distribute the milk, you must go to mass during lent every morning before school without eating beforehand so you can receive holy communion at 5:30 am, you must walk there alone then school will begin, you must not be hungry you must not notice that Janice already has breasts and when she pledges allegiance she puts her right hand right on her left breast, we all laugh about it, since you are so smart you must take over when I have to leave the room, you must put all the names of the boys who are bad on the blackboard in order: Eugene LeRoc, James Noeth, John Hoefferle. Here is another new child from Germany, she cant speak English, we must help her alot, German is not a good language to speak in this world. I love you, said Sister Roseanna, please let me love you, you are the only person who understands me and now I will tell you all about my life and my feelings. I hate you, said Sister Teresa, come with me to Seton Hall, I require a lay companion to go to my classes, to travel with me. Now you are expelled from the Boy Saviour Moment because you were at Freddy Steigel's party where everyone kissed each other and you do not get a green mark meaning good on your card but a bad red mark meaning bad for every day since you played kissing games, please stand in the back of the room everyone who was at the kissing party. Bernadette, I'm most surprised at you I thought you were so smart besides I hate you so I thought you were so good and I have a dread disease which is killing me, see my little bent fingers, you can tell this disease is killing me and it's all your fault. Sister Joseph left because she was sick too, enough that she was nicer, kinder than Sister Teresa. My mother said see I have breast cancer it is killing me because you punched me in the breasts, my father died suddenly, Father Joseph was there at the house when he died. Do you want to look at him? He vomited before he died. I didnt look at him. My uncle said I will take care of you, a weird remark, you'll see later. I went to see Father Sylvian, he said you are lovely, come here. I went to a retreat and met Father Wilson, a friend of my uncle's. He said we who advocated free love, that was me Grace and Fran, ought to kneel down and beg forgiveness, then he pushed his erection into our faces begging us to suck him off. By that time my mother had died, addicted to morphine and refusing a second operation. She was helpless and moaned in the night. It was torture to take care of her. Daytimes toward the end a woman named Frances would come and take care of her. She was reading odd books like mystery novels, I began a novena to St. Jude, patron saint of hopeless cases or causes, I told her in the hospital that intravenous feeding would make her well not knowing what else to say, she was emaciated and begged me at age 13 not to let her die in a hospital, I came home one day and found her whisked off again to the hospital, there to die on xmas eve, I receiving an emergency phone call that she was very sick they said, we went to the hospital and saw her dead, a big black death had dripped from her mouth, my sister and I hugged each other horribly for the last time in years. She was rigid. When my father died someone took us out immediately and bought us a record player and some records including a Ricky Nelson album. To distract us. When my mother died no such thing happened. We had to go through another funeral and wake, we had to put up on xmas eve the little monster characters that were the nativity scene in our catholic home where from time to time a box full of a statue like coming out of a crypt was sent home from school so we could say the family rosary around it while watching Bishop Sheen. When my father died, I'd been looking all morning after church, it was a Sunday, October 20th, at dirty magazines in the candy store with one of my boyfriends. I thought for many years that was the reason he died. Left all alone in the stodgy nightmare of lifeless fear of death, my sister and I continued to live "downstairs" in the two family house of our origins. Upstairs lived our grandfather and our now coping uncle, who was more or less in charge of us. He was a bachelor of the most extreme sort, he had piles of religious magazines on the floor of his "hall bedroom" which is the room in this sort of house that hovers over the downstairs hallway, it is an inevitably small room and his magazines were arranged by him, an impecunious person, that too but what I mean is an obsessive endomorph, in the order in which he had not read them. He was a lunatic and he was now our caretaker. He had a large head and a small body, he was the only person in our family who had ever gone to college—to become a certified public accountant. My mother, before she died, exhorted us not to go to college so as not to try to "rise up out of your class." Our relatives hated us and would not consider taking care of us now that we were orphans. I overheard one of their conversations about it in which my Aunt Ellie (father's sister) said "we dont want them and neither does anybody else." My mother, whose name was also Marie, was always considered to be a snotty person because for one thing she was good-looking and for another, as families go, I think my father's family thought she thought she was better than they were because of some kind of Germany that was called high and another kind of Germany that was called low. Also my father's family was probably secretly Jewish though no one would ever admit to this; they came from Alsace Lorraine, via other places. Being in my uncle's care was no picnic. He was a man living as they said then in the single state of blessedness. When my sister took up with some interesting men including Vito Acconci and all the men he was then going to college with at Holy Cross in Worcester, they would come over late at night and often stay. Peter Lupario would court me undiligently and try to induce me to listen to the folk music station. We discovered that our dead parents had a stash of Chivas Regal and other liquors which we drank and became drunk on. Often at five in the morning the men would hide in the built-in closets in my mother's former bedroom so that our grandfather, when he brought in the milk, wouldnt know they were there. We also danced wildly but hardly ever made love. I dont know what my uncle was thinking but he would have wild fights which we could hear with my grandfather about sharing steaks and the other problems of bachelor lives. When my sister married Vito I had to be the maid of honor. They left for Iowa and I was left with the alternative of either going to a catholic school or going to a catholic school. I begged to keep the downstairs apartment and go to Hunter but my uncle felt he couldn't be in charge of me and only if I lived upstairs with him could I go to a non-catholic school. I was going out with a man four years older than I was though he was short of stature. Since my mother had died I had worked at St. Vincent's Hospital on weekends and in the summertime and as a result had been cruising the village for understanding. I had become a little bit beat, had marched in marches and spent unbeknownst to anyone a lot of time waiting at Patchin Place for a sight of e.e.cummings. I took the Canarsie Line to St. Vincent's from Ridgewood and many times on the train I had been harrassed and attacked by men or boys but I had never been hurt by them and never told anyone about it. There was a nurse at St. Vincent's, a Sister Richard, who took a great liking to me, she was a very fat woman, and placed me in an office by myself and gave me all her duties as head nurse to perform, so I did all her paperwork and got to know for the first time in my life a rich young woman who lived on Washington Square North in what I thought of as a very beautiful house. We went there together often at lunchtimes. After my sister left, my uncle got more and more nuts. He would stand at the foot of my bed in the upstairs apartment where I was on weekends which was right next to the wall of my grandfather's room through which I could hear him moaning and being old and he, my uncle Andrew would say to me like a suitor, what would you like to do today, always holding in his arms a bunch of Saturday laundry. Can I take you somewhere? We would go on long walks, always ending up at the gigantic German res-

taurant where there had been all the meals after funerals, Geb-
hardt's, and my uncle would consume prime ribs of beef and
ask me if I would like to proceed to pay a visit, on foot, to the
cemetery. I remembered always when I was at Gebhardt's with
my parents their telling me not to drink the delicious amber
glass of water that was offered at the beginning of the meal lest
I should then be unable to eat enough afterwards to justify the
cost of the dinners. I remember the dressed-up smell of the
place. From Gebhardt's it was not a long walk to the cemetery
and the relation of the eating to the deaths was rapidly made
though it did not need to be. Then we would make the long
walk back like lovers up Fresh Pond Road, my uncle and me,
and stop at a brand new Carvel that'd just opened to get some
sweet thing which was supposed to please me but did not.
What pleased me was my uncle's love, stupid as it was, his
attention, his crazy devotion, his merest repentance when he
said to me, "I knew I was always waiting and saving myself to
marry you." He knew much more than I did I would guess. He
asked me to help him choose socks that would match his ties
for the next day. He died in his tiny hall bedroom bed at the
same early age as my parents at a moment when I was visiting
my lover at Cornell, it was Easter Sunday and it was the same
day my mother had been born, his sister. My lover was scared
of airplanes so we took buses from Ithaca, stopping off at some
scary place like Albany where we drank tea and coffee, I had
been living on a diet of grilled cheese sandwiches and tea for a
long time then and couldnt understand, cause I didnt know
there was caffeine in tea or nurture in food, why I could never
sleep or live, why I was so scared of everything and so tired. I
got to my uncle's wake and remember standing in the bath-
room of the funeral home talking to my girlfriends and then I

suddenly said I dont think I can stand up anymore. I was taken away, finally to some hospital, after great turmoil about who— nobody among my fearful relatives would do it, thinking me or us jinxed—would admit me formally to the place. They must've though I would die too like all the other members of my family but I didnt. I was diagnosed as having Lupus dis- seminatus but I didnt have anything but an unallayed grief. I had been in a catholic women's college for one year at this time and there I felt like an outcast only able to make friends with a brilliant dour young nun who liked to massage me while talk- ing about Shelley and with some of the richest women in the school. I went to dinners at their houses which shocked me because I was supposed to ring a buzzer under my part of the table when I wanted something and then the maid would come and ask what and bring it, that friend of mine was related to Cardinal Spellman, and boy did they have wine cellars, but I think much of that happened the year after my uncle died, right before I was informally thrown out for wearing sandals and openly reading Freud when I became most angry and wouldn't perform on the intramural basketball team for the lesbian gym teachers and just sat on the sidelines because I loved them very much and hoped they loved me too. The same teachers taught us swimming and we had competitions about who looked best in her bathing suit which was just a black tank suit and just a joke and we had competitions later about who could best imi- tate a man making love to a woman and teach the girls who didnt know.

ESSAY: HOW CAREFULLY DO WE TEND?

How carefully do we tend, paper white narcissuses?
Ashen the blossoms or pure white bulbs
I like that guy, hell he's a horse's ass
Like a modern day Madame Bovary the androgyne of literary
      history
No vision vision of the succinct bomb to all
A pretty orderly home wracked with cancerous pain
The image of a beautiful young woman foreseen with saddest
      eyes & in a different body
If I make the delicious custard it will be filled with splinters
The person who helps me sell my Grecian vases takes half the
      money
I love my fantastic toys of breathless unburnable plastic
I wish I were Shakespeare so I could be rich
And thought is thought he said only for those who think
When you become wiser you'll see you had been prettier in the
      past

& when you didnt know it you were wise
Your dead or former lover fills you with desire
You move the bed back into the dining room again
& eat no meat but only mashed potatoes since you still have
       teeth & the guts for philosophy
You do not learn Chinese but Christian melodies in Chinese
       class
The Spanish you are taught is said to be not Castilian
Your punk shoes were made in Korea
Your expensive art supplies are replaced by cheap computers
In your competitive classes where pure knowledge is unseemly
The bookcases you got from Gothic Cabinet Craft fall down
You are told they arent meant to hold so many books
The concept of separation is encouraged by the marriage coun-
       selors
Much to the dismay of their still coherent clients
The expensive eye doctor at 10 Downing Street creates
A visually ugly surrounding for his patients
The idealistic lawyer is forced to demand
A hundred dollars an hour for his time
The new glasses the eye doctor makes for you
Create mountains in the pavement & bulges in the straight
       glass door
You yourself are strait but yet you are gay
Or let me put it another way, you have always been gay
But you have had to be strait, often it was hard to know the
       difference
Between a liberal and a conservative, yet you tried to fathom
Why your highschool friends who were for Kennedy both be-
       longed to the Young Americans for Freedom and
Marched in the ban the bomb marches at the same time as

They were fighting for independence for Northern Ireland
I really dont know what's in even the freshest bread
I've got a lease so what causes my daily alarm?
Why panic I when friends give me their artworks
To hang on the battered walls we agreed would make landlords
     eternal plasterers in the inferno
Why jump I so? It's fun to jump
Was there going to be yet a big jump? Did we learn without a
     teacher?
Does the heat of the broken inventions preclude a fire?
Will I be lucky this week? Will it not snow till the day it does?
Will my sister finally win the lottery?
Will love arrive with poetry in a cart? Will lovers
Assume their proper roles before the New Year? Will artists
Begin to study again and deny the commercial? Will the
     schools
Ever begin to stand for the love of people for their children?
Can even the good-looking vegetables be trusted?
What shall we eat? Health-food puffed millet?
What will the weather be like tomorrow? Will I ever see you
     again?

NATHANIEL HAWTHORNE

CONCLUSION

After a while, enough time had gone by for people to arrange their sentences about the scene that I have described & then there was more than one version of what had been seen on the scaffold.

And most of them testified, most of them said they had seen a scarlet letter on the breast of the priest. And it was the same one the *she* wore but this one was printed, was imbedded in the flesh of the man. And where it came from was all that was left to talk about & all this was done in a logical way. Some of the one who were talking said that the priest, the same day she first wore her letter, began to wear his, or at least wear his into himself—something about penance, a method of penance, or many methods, some kind of strange torture, the presence of the letter in the flesh. And some of the ones who were talking, these others said that the sign of the letter had not been produced until much later, when the old shaman & lover of the dead had made it appear, in an amazing regression, through the use of magic words & poisonous drugs. And others again—& these were the ones who knew the priest best, understood his lability & studied psychoanalysis—they whispered their belief that the insistence of the letter in the mind of the priest caused it to grow steadily outward, finally manifesting the judgement of memory in the own body of the man by the visible presence of the letter. You can choose among these theories. We have talked all we can about meaning & we'd gladly, now that it's played its part, erase the print of the letter from our own brain. We've thought too much about it, it's become too distinct.

But it's odd, anyway, that some of the people who saw this whole scene & said that they never looked away, some denied that there was any mark at all on the breast of the priest, as if he were a baby. And, according to these people, his dying words never said, they didnt imply any, even the slightest connection, for him, with the guilt for which she had worn the letter. And according to these same people, the priest, conscious that he was dying, & conscious also that his sainthood had been preserved, has shown his desire, by dying in the arms of someone openly guilty to express to the world how worthless & stupid the ideas, of right & wrong are. And so he was an angel. After spending his life in the way that he had, he had made his death some sort of lesson for his audience, that, in any view that encompasses everything, we are really all the same. And it was to teach them, somehow, that the best readers & writers were just so far above any others as to see the little you need to know to get rid of any idea of value at all. Without arguing such an amazing truth, we have to consider this version of his story as just an example of that enraged faith with which a man's friends will sometimes defend him, when proofs, clear as the sun on the character of the letter, establish him a false one & just as confused as anyone else.

The authority we've been using—an old manuscript drawn up from people's verbal testimony—says all these things, & some of these people had known her & other ones had just heard the story from her own contemporaries. A moral becomes a pressure at this point—the priest's experience leads nowhere. This is the only moral we will make a sentence out of: it's Poe's "My Heart Laid Bare" again, it's "Show freely to the world, somehow, if not the worst & the truth is not just the worst, but anyway, show something from which we can infer the worst, deal with the worst, or maybe, just show, something, anything."

Nothing was more amazing than the change that happened, almost immediately after the priest's death, in the looks & attitude of an old shaman. All his strength & energy, all his comceptual & intellectual force, his power seemed to desert him almost completely; in fact he withered, he withered up, he shrivelled away, he was vanishing, he was vanishing into thin air, he was going up in smoke, he was ceasing to be, almost vanishing from sight, like an uprooted tree that leaves many branches behind, that leaves not a branch behind. This fantastic man had made the whole center of his life the study & systematic exercise of revenge through transference; and when, by its complete triumph & consummation in the total reorganization of the employment of faculties in the mind of the priest, when that, in this case evil principle was left with no more material to work on, nothing to support him or it, when, in short, there was no more devil's work on earth for him to do, all that was left for the dehumanized man was to find himself a new master of his own, another shaman, & work for him & get paid. but toward all these shadow people, these introjections we've just begun to understand—all the others & even the shaman himself—we might just as well feel an attitude of beneficent neutrality, a simple fascination. It's a curious subject of observation in any inquiry or analysis, whether hatred & love are the same in the end. Each, when its pushed that far, supposes an incredible intimacy & heart-knowledge; each renders one person dependent on another for both food & fame, existing in a state of symbiosis; the passions of the lover & the passions of the one who hates create an anxiety of the same force when the subject is withdrawn, the anxiety of separation, loss of the possibility of mutuality. So, looked at this way, love & hatred seem the same, except that one happens to be seen in the light of desire for strength in a stronger existence, and the other is a lurid distortion of this, as the repetition of a dead desire. In some other world, the old curer & the priest—mutual victims as they have been—may, without knowing it, have found what they made of their hatred changed into love, their stock of baser metals transmuted into gold, & may in fact have discovered, these mutual victims, the elixir of perpetual youth.

But forgetting all this, there is some information you should have. When the old doctor died, which he did within the year, his rescue fantasies did not cease, and by his last will & testament, of which some of the ones who were mentioned before were executors, he left an enormous amount of property, both here & in England, to Pearl, the daughter of Hester Prynne.

So the elf-child, child-wife, the demon offspring, as some people, even up to that point, continued to call her, became the richest heiress of her day in the new spirit. Pretty predictably, this circumstance changed everbody's mind; and, had the

mother & child stayed here, the demon child, after adoles-
cence, might have mingled her wild blood with the blood of the
most puritanical of them all. But, in no time after the doctor's
death, the bearer of the scarlet letter disappeared, and the child
along with her. For years, though every once in a while some
vague story would find its way across the sea—like a shapeless
object carved with the initial letter of some name—still no real
word was heard. And the story of the scarlet letter was a
history. But its magic never lost power, and kept the scaffold
where the priest died awful & the house by the sea where the
others had lived, this was invested with magic. Near this spot,
one afternoon, some children were playing, when they saw a
tall woman in a gray robe come up to the door of the house by
the sea. In all those years it had never once been opened; but
either she unlocked it, or the decaying wood & iron fell at the
touch of her hand, or, or she went as a shadow though any
impediment—but, in any event, she went in.

She stopped in the doorway & turned partly around—
maybe, the idea of going alone & so changed into the space of
an old life & an intense one, was more than even she could
bear. But her hesitation only lasted long enough to show the
color of the letter on her breast as a point of light.

So she had returned, she had resumed, something about
guilt. And if the child was still alive, she must have been a
woman by now. No one knew, or ever learned for sure,
whether the elf-child had survived or in what direction a wild-
ness like hers could go in the world. But, for the rest of Hes-
ter's life, there were indications that the recluse of the scarlet
letter was the object of love & interest from some inhabitant of
another world. Letters came, with armorial seals upon them,
but they were bearings unknown to English heraldry. And in

the house there were such amazing things that no one could ever use them & only incredible wealth could provide them, & love imagine them. There were small books too, ornamented books, designed books, bespeaking a continual remembrance, that must have been made in editions of only one. And once Hester was seen embroidering clothes for a baby & she was using all the colors, she was using so many colors that any baby would have been a whole scandal appearing in these clothes in our monochrome community.

In the end, the gossip of the day was—and the man who made investigations a century later believed—and one of his recent successors in office believes—and I believe—that Pearl was not alive, but rich & happy & would have been glad to share that whole life with her mother.

But there was something else for Hester Prynne to do here, in New England, and not in that unknown region where Pearl was living now. Here had been the origins of her desire; here its completion & its distortion & the working out of that; her real work was still to be done & it had to be done here. She had returned, she had resumed—and freely, for even the sternest authority of that iron period would never have imposed it—resumed the outward symbol of what this whole story has been telling. She never abandoned it again, it was always visible. But, in the lapse of the years that made up her life, the scarlet letter ceased to be a stigma which attracted the world's abnormal scorn & bitterness at a broken taboo, and became a type of something to be looked at & studied, sometimes with awe, an amazing sign of something about the future, or the progression of time itself, the insistence of the letter in the unconscious. Some people worshipped it, in a peculiar way. And, as Hester Prynne had an investment in understanding human behavior, people began to know this & brought all their troubles & confusions, and sought her as a counsellor, as one who had herself gone through an amazing struggle. Women especially—in the continually recurring instances of wounded, wasted, wronged, misplaced, or erring & unaccepted love—or with the incredible burden of love withheld because it was unvalued or not sought out—came to her house by the sea, demanding why they were so unhappy & what was the cure! Hester comforted & counselled them with the methods she knew. She assured them, too, of her firm belief, that, at some brighter period, when the world should have grown ripe for it, when people understood enough, a new truth would be revealed, in order to establish the whole relation between man & woman on a surer ground of mutual happiness. Earlier in life, Hester had imagined that she herself might be the destined prophetess of this sexual & psychological revolution, but she had long since recognized the impossibility that any mission such as this should be done by one woman, especially one burdened with what she still considered a life-long sorrow, a life-long guilt. The angel of the coming revelation must be woman indeed, but direct & wise, and not through grief; and this at least was his fantasy: she would be showing how love & sex should make us happy or sublime by the creation of a true science in a life successful to such a end!

So said Hester Prynne, and glanced her sad eyes downward at the scarlet letter. And, after many years a new grave was delved, near an old & sunken one, in that burial-ground beside which King's Chapel has since been built. It was near that old & sunken grave, yet with a space between, as if the dust of the two sleepers had no right to mingle. Yet one tombstone served for both. All around, there were monuments carved with armorial bearings; and on this simple slab of slate—as the curious investigator may still discern, and perplex himself with the purport—there appeared the semblance of an engraved escutcheon. It bore a device, a herald's wording of which might serve for a motto & brief description of our now concluded legend; so sombre is it, & relieved only by one ever-glowing point of light gloomier than the shadow:—

"ON A FIELD, SABLE, THE LETTER A, GULES."

NOTES

An *escutcheon* is a shield or shield-shaped surface on which a coat of arms is displayed. (A "blot on one's es-cuteheon" is a stain on one's honor, disgrace to one's reputation) . . . "the semblance of an engraved escutcheon."

A *field,* in heraldry, is the surface or part of the surface of a shield.

A *herald* (abbr. *her.*) is an English official in charge of genealogies & heraldic arms, and a person who proclaims or announces significant news, a messenger, someone who comes before to announce, to give indication of what is to come: "a herald's wording"; a forerunner, harbinger, someone who foretells, who ushers in; "the angel of the coming revolution (revelation)."

Sable, in heraldry, is the color black, represented in engraving by crossing vertical & horizontal lines to produce a dark shading. "So somber is it, & relieved only by one ever-glowing point of light gloomier than the shadow": *THE LET-TER A*

Gules, in heraldry, is the color red indicated in black & white engravings by parallel vertical lines: "yet with a space between, as if the dust of the two sleepers had no right to mingle." *Gules* originates from Old French for red-dyed ermine, originally the plural of the word for mouth, deriving from the latin *gula,* throat.

Sables are a neckpiece or coat made of the fur or pelt of the sable, sables are mourning clothes, black. The *sable* is a flesh-eating weasel-like mammal of northern Europe & Asia valued for its dark black fur.

The *ermine* is any of several weasels of northern regions, whose fur is brown in summer but white with a black-tipped tail in winter. The soft white fur of the ermine is used to trim the necks of women's coats. In European countries a judge's state robe is trimmed with ermine as an emblem of honor & purity. *Ermines,* in heraldry, indicates the representation of fur, consisting of a white field with black spots: "On a field, sable, the letter A, gules."